MARIAMA BÂ catapulted i her
first novel, *So Long a Letter* nd
admiration. The Senegalese w ;al,
in 1929, was educated 'unlike .on'
at the École Normale for gi .que. She was raised as a
Muslim by maternal grandparents.

Bâ began writing at school and in her early essays there are
hints at the critical approach to society that she was to adopt in her
later writing. A pioneer of women's rights, she became involved in
several Senegalese women's organisations. Her commitment to erad-
icating inequalities between men and women in Africa led her to
write *So Long a Letter*. The novel, originally written in French, was
translated into sixteen languages and won the first Noma Award for
Publishing in Africa. The English translation of the novel was first
published in 1981.

A schoolteacher and inspector by profession, Bâ promoted the
crucial role of the writer in Africa. She believed that the 'sacred
mission' of the writer was to strike out 'at the archaic practices,
traditions and customs that are not a real part of our precious
cultural heritage'. *So Long a Letter* succeeds admirably in its mission.

Bâ died tragically in 1981 in Dakar after a long illness, just
before her second novel *Le Chant Écarlate* appeared.

KENNETH HARROW is a professor of English with specialisa-
tions in African literature and cinema, post colonialism, feminism
and African diaspora studies. He was a Fulbright Professor at the
University of Yaoundé, from 1977–79, a Fulbright Research Scholar
in Dakar from 1982–3 and a Senior Fulbright Professor there from
2005 to 2006. His publications include *Thresholds of Change in African
Literature* (Heinemann, 1994), *Less Than One and Double: A Feminist
Reading of African Women's Writing* (Heinemann, 2002 – a French
translation was published by L'Harmattan in 2007), and he has
edited numerous collections on such topics as Islam and African
literature, African cinema and women in African cinema. His latest
book, *Postcolonial African Cinema*, was published in 2007 by Indiana
University Press.

MARIAMA BÂ

SO LONG A LETTER

TRANSLATED FROM THE FRENCH
BY MODUPÉ BODÉ-THOMAS

INTRODUCTION BY KENNETH W. HARROW

Heinemann

Heinemann is an imprint of Pearson Education Limited, a company incorporated
in England and Wales, having its registered office at Edinburgh Gate, Harlow,
Essex, CM20 2JE. Registered company number: 872828

www.africanwriters.com

Heinemann is a registered trademark of Pearson Education Limited

© Les Nouvelles Editions Africaines 1980
© In translation Modupé Bodé-Thomas 1981
Introduction © Kenneth W. Harrow 2008

First published by Les Nouvelles Editions Africaines 1980
First published in the African Writers Series 1981
This edition published by Pearson Education Limited 2008

12 11 10 09 08
10 9 8 7 6 5 4 3 2

British Library Cataloguing in Publication Data.
A catalogue record for this book is available from the British Library.

ISBN 978 0 435913 52 6

Copyright notice

Typeset by Sara Rafferty
Cover design by Tony Richardson
Cover artwork from original by John Montgomery
Author photograph by George Hallett
Printed by CPI Cox & Wyman, Reading, RG1 8EX

Acknowledgements

Every effort has been made to contact copyright holders of material reproduced in
this book. Any omissions will be rectified in subsequent printings if notice is given
to the publishers.

INTRODUCTION

When Mariama Bâ's *So Long a Letter* appeared in 1979, it was one of the first novels by a Senegalese woman in French,[1] and in a sense became one of the foundational texts for Francophone women writers. It was the first African novel to win the prestigious Noma award in 1980.

Written as a semi-autobiographical account, its protagonist Ramatoulaye is a woman who came of age during the period of late colonialism, married a Senegalese nationalist and gave birth to twelve children as their country passed into independence. She faced her husband's rejection and then his death as the country experienced the passage from colony to modern nation.

Both the intimacy of its address and its turn to the epistolary mode[2] marked *So Long a Letter* as a unique form of fiction writing in contemporary African women's literature. Moreover, it broke new ground as a deeply personal account of the trials that are peculiar to the Muslim Senegalese woman of today. Ramatoulaye sets out the story of her present tribulations, the past events that led up to them, and the anxieties she faces as a mother, in a series of letters to her 'sister' Aissatou, who herself faced the trauma of a long-term marriage coming to an end as her husband chose to take a young woman as his second wife. Ramatoulaye and Aissatou evoke the situation of the mature, troubled woman, of those who have only each other to turn to for sustenance. As such Aissatou

---

1 Four years earlier, Nafissatou Diallo had published her autobiography, *A Dakar Childhood*. In 1976, Aminata Sow Fall had published *Le Revenant* and in 1979 *The Beggars' Strike*.

2 See Christopher Miller's brilliant analysis of the novel, and especially its unique role as an epistolary novel, in *Theories of Africans* (1990). In fact, this form, common to novels of the eighteenth century, is extremely rare in African literature.

functions as the interlocutor of Ramatoulaye's letters, standing in the place of the reader who shares in the accounts presented in the letters. The reader's place is defined by this address of mature sister to sister, of Senegalese woman to Senegalese woman, and thus is brought into an intimate, private space created by Bâ.

Until this point in African literature, the portrayal of such women was primarily presented as that of women's 'plight,' that is, as victims like those appearing in the fiction written by Senegalese men. They were seen in such films as *Xala* (1974) by Sembène Ousmane, with the epitome of this figure being El Hadj's ever-patient first wife, Adja Awa Astou. The novels by other African women writers like Flora Nwapa, Buchi Emecheta and Ama Ata Aidoo also often emphasized the images of women abandoned by their husbands, maltreated by their fathers, or even, as in *The Joys of Motherhood* (1979), ultimately ignored by their own grown children. Women were represented as disempowered or abused. The African feminist voice had not yet posed the question of how to speak beyond the confines of the suffering voice, how to give an account of the fuller life in which a woman – as first a child, then a wife, a mother and a widow – could embody all the complexities of a life confronted with courage and faith, as well as one marked by despair. *So Long a Letter* makes possible the novels of Ken Bugul, Nafissatou Diallo and Catherine N'Diaye who aspired to convey new visions of the woman's experience, especially in terms of the project of defining the New African Woman within the space of a new order of modernity.

For Ramatoulaye, 'modernity' began with the colonial period. As a child she was one of the first girls to attend the French school, and for her the experience had much that was exhilarating. Her French teacher is described as having 'love' for her charges without 'patronizing' them. These included Ramatoulaye, Aissatou and their classmates, 'with our plaits either standing on end or bent down, with our loose blouses, our wrappers. She knew how to discover and appreciate our qualities' (16). Bâ's judgement of the colonial school stands in radical opposition to those voiced by the anticolonial, national liberationist authors of the 1950s and 1960s who saw in the colonial educational institutions an extension of the repressive mechanisms of the colonial enterprise. For Ramatoulaye, the path chosen for the girls' training by their head-mistress 'has not been at all fortuitous. It has accorded with the profound choices made by New Africa for the promotion of the black woman' (16). Thus she judges her generation to be 'the first pioneers of the promotion of African women' (15).

The New African is ostensibly the one who has opted for a modern path of development. Partly 'New Africa' is seen as independent Africa; partly 'New Africa' implies passing beyond the old traditional ways. This was the choice put by the Grand Royal to the Diallobe people in Cheikh Hamidou Kane's *Ambiguous Adventure* (1961), when she urges her people to make the heart-rending decision to learn the white man's ways so as to avoid remaining under his domination forever. It is the choice whose negative consequences might be seen in the eventual breakdown suffered by Samba Diallo in *Ambiguous Adventure*, with his apparent suicide at the end of his itinerary to modernism. For Kane, this passage to modernity through Europe led away from the Truth of an Islamic way of life. It is also the path of loss of integrity Sem-bène traces in the character of Ndeye in *God's Bits of Wood* (1960).

In case after case, from Mongo Beti's *Mission to Kala* (1957) or Ferdinand Oyono's *Houseboy* (1956) to Jean-Marie Teno's more recent film *Afrique, je te plumerai* (1992), the loss engendered by acculturation to European ways forms the subject of an anticolonial literature. However, it is also the path to liberation that Flora Nwapa traces in her own autobiographical account, *Women Are Different* (1986), as a Nigerian girl attending a British school in the colonial period. In so much of African women's literature, as with Nafissatou Diallo's *A Dakar Childhood* (1975) or

Buchi Emecheta's *Head above Water* (1986), the modernist path for the New African Woman was not defined simply by taking control of the newly independent state, a process entirely dominated by men, who emerged as the new rulers and often remained, as with El Hadj Abdou Kader Beye in *Xala*, the old patriarchs. As the date of publication of *So Long a Letter* (1979) indicates, independence for the New African Woman came a full generation after independence of the African state.

Bâ's espousal of modernism entailed a project of liberation for women that had had to defer to the men's project of achieving national liberation. This project for women's liberation still engenders great conflict in North Africa. But in sub-Saharan Africa its time has clearly come, and *So Long a Letter* played a not inconsiderable role in effecting this change, especially in Senegal.

Senegal is a Muslim country, and the issue of negotiating the passage to modernity without renouncing a Muslim identity has been at the heart of much Senegalese literature from the outset, as seen especially in *Ambiguous Adventure*, as well as the early works of Abdoulaye Sadji, Ousmane Socé, Sembène Ousmane, and the philosophical and historical texts of Mamadou Dia. For Bâ it was important to establish Ramatoulaye's adherence to an identity as a practising Muslim woman at the outset. The novel begins with an account of the death of Ramatoulaye's estranged husband, Modou, but it is thirty-five pages before we learn of their estrangement. Instead, we are immersed in the practice of *mirasse*, the period of mourning and seclusion for widows, during which all the faults of the deceased are to be brought to light – hence the letters to Aissatou.[3] However, in the course of the accounting Ramatoulaye

3 This process of disclosing the faults of the person who died was closely analysed by Mbye Cham in his seminal article on *So Long a Letter*, 'Contemporary Society and the Female Imagination: A Study of the Novels of Mariama Bâ.' *Women in African Literature Today*. 15 (1987), 89–101.

does much more than focus on the flaws of her faithless husband, or recall their earlier, more hopeful years in the past. She evokes most forcefully her deep distress as a believer, as a faithful wife and companion to Modou, but also her social and religious obligations as a daughter-in-law, sister-in-law, and now widow. She does not challenge the order that imposes those obligations, even though she sees herself having been liberated as a child, because she did not see such a path of liberation as conflicting with the social conventions of the Senegalese Muslim traditions. It is not too much to say that this definition of the correct urban citizen was 'new' or 'modern' only to the extent that it left intact most of the architecture of the family and religion. Only at the periphery of the society, in matters concerning education, dress and social comportment, would the pressures of modernization come into conflict with the imperatives of older customs and values.

These conflicting pressures are accentuated as Ramatoulaye loses her husband, first to a younger woman and then to death, and finds herself alone and widowed, obliged to deal with her family on her own. At first, she is forced to confront a series of suitors, beginning with her husband's elder brother Tamsir, who expects to make her another one of his wives. As she responds forcefully to him, we hear the expression of a new passion, a new voice: 'My voice has known thirty years of silence, thirty years of harassment. It bursts out, violent, sometimes sarcastic, sometimes contemptuous' (60). She rejects both his offer and his arrogant assumption of male superiority, and she puts in their place the brother, the suitor and the imam, along with all the former prerogatives of the patriarchal order that attempted to assert its control over her again.

As her gradual passage from wife to widow yields to the pressures of single motherhood, she comes to confront the dangers of modernism to which her children are exposed. She catches three of her daughters smoking, she has to deal with her sons recklessly playing in the street, and finally, most movingly, must handle the delicate situation posed by her daughter Aissatou's pregnancy.

It is at this point that Ramatoulaye passes from being the maltreated victim of male indifference to being the autonomous parent whose reactions and values are to shape the life of her child profoundly. As she struggles as a mother over how to treat her daughter in need, the dictates of religion and traditional custom, and issues of becoming the New African Woman, fade into the background. Ramatoulaye tells us that at this point she seeks refuge in God, but in the end decides to act on the basis of her feelings as a mother.

> One is a mother so as to face the flood. Was I to threaten, in the face of my daughter's shame, her sincere repentance, her pain, her anguish? Was I?
>
> I took my daughter in my arms. Painfully, I held her tightly, with a force multiplied tenfold by pagan revolt and primitive tenderness. (88)

In the final chapters of *So Long a Letter*, Ramatoulaye turns increasingly to the dicta of her grandmother. From generations of foremothers to those of their daughters, to her own situation as soon-to-be-grandmother, she embraces her fate as the woman of her times, forcefully forging the image of the 'New African Woman' whose trajectory is delineated by the choices she makes based on both tenderness and revolt. Aissatou's financial success and career might have been thought to qualify her as the exemplar for the position of the New African Woman. But with Rama-toulaye Bâ reminds us of the importance of values grounded in Senegalese ways, which account for the strengths of this most enduring figure and for the considerable influence that this novel has had upon subsequent generations of African women.

Kenneth W. Harrow
East Lansing, Michigan, 2008

FOR FURTHER REFERENCE

Novels by Mariama Bâ

Un Chant écarlate. Dakar: Les Nouvelles Editions Africaines, 1981. Translated as *Scarlet Song*. Trans. Dorothy S. Blair. Harlow; New York: Longman, 1985.

Une si longue lettre. Dakar: Les Nouvelles Editions Africaines, 1979. Translated as *So Long a Letter*. Trans. Modupé Bodé-Thomas. London: Heinemann, 1981.

Interviews

Bâ, Mariama. 'Mariama Bâ, Winner of the First Noma Award for Publishing in Africa.' Interview by Barbara Harrell-Bond. *African Publishing Record*. 6 (1980), 209–14.

Relevant novels by other authors

Beti, Mongo. *Mission terminée*, Paris: Buchet Chastel, 1957. Translated as *Mission to Kala*. Trans. Peter Green. London: Heinemann Educational, 1964.

Bugul, Ken. *Le Baobab fou*. Dakar: Les Nouvelles Editions Africaines, 1984.

Diallo, Nafissatou. *De Tilène au Plateau*. Darak: Les Nouvelles Editions Africaines, 1975. Translated as *A Dakar Childhood*. Trans. Dorothy S. Blair. Harlow: Longman, 1982.

Emecheta, Buchi. *The Joys of Motherhood*. London: Heinemann, 1979. *Head above Water*. London: Ogwugwo Afo, 1986.

Fall, Aminata Sow. *La grève des bàttu, ou, Les déchets humains*. Dakar: Nouvelles Editions Africaines, 1976. Translated as *The beggars' strike, or, The dregs of society*. Trans. Dorothy S. Blair. Harlow, Essex: Longman Longman, 1981.

Le Revenant. Dakar: Les Nouvelles Editions Africaines, 1979.

Kane, Cheikh Hamidou. *L'aventure ambiguë*. Paris: Juillard, 1961. Translated as *Ambiguous Adventure* (1961) Trans. Katherine Wood. New York: Walker, 1963.

Nwapa, Flora. *Women Are Different*. Enugu, Nigeria: Tana Press, 1986.

Oyono, Ferdinand. *Une Vie de Boy*. Paris: Julliard, 1956. Translated as *Houseboy*. (1958) Trans. John Reed. London: Heinemann, 1966.

Sembène Ousmane. *Les bouts de bois de Dieu*. Paris: Le Livre Contemporain, 1960. Translated as *God's Bits of Wood*. (1960) Trans. Francis Price. London: Heinemann, 1962.

Films

Sembène Ousmane (Dir.). *Xala* (1974).

Teno, Jean-Marie (Dir.). *Afrique, je te plumerai* (1992).

Critical Studies of Bâ

d'Almeida, Irene Assiba. 'The Concept of Choice in Mariama Bâ's Fiction.' *Ngambika: Studies of Women in African Literature*. Ed. Carole Boyce Davies and Anne Adams Graves. Trenton, NJ: Africa World Press, 1986, 161–171.

Azodo, Ada Uzoamaka, Ed. *Emerging perspectives on Mariama Bâ: postcolonialism, feminism, and postmodernism*. Trenton, NJ: Africa World Press, 2003.

Cham, Mbye B. 'Contemporary Society and the Female Imagination: A Study of the Novels of Mariama Bâ.' *African Literature Today*, 15 (1987), 89–101.

'The Female Condition in Africa: A Literary Exploration by Mariama Bâ.' *Current Bibliography on African Affairs*, 17.1 (1984–5), 29–51.

Champagne, John. ''A Feminist Just Like Us?' Teaching Mariama Bâ's *So Long a Letter*.' *College English*, 58:1 (1996 Jan), 22–42.

Edson, Laurie. 'Mariama Bâ and the Politics of the Family.' *Studies in Twentieth Century Literature*, 17.1 (1993), 13–25.

Esonwanne, Uzo. 'Enlightenment Epistemology and 'Aesthetic Cognition': Mariama Ba's *So Long a Letter*.' *The Politics of (M)othering: Identity and Resistance in African Literature*. Ed. Obioma Nnaemeka. New York: Routledge, 1997, 82–100.

Halling, Kirsten. 'Negotiating the Crossroads between Tradition and Modernity: Cinematic and Visual Imagery in Mariama Bâ's *Une Si Longue Lettre*.' *Essays in French Literature*, 40 (2003 Nov), 81–102.

Irlam, Shaun. 'Mariama Bâ's *Une Si Longue Lettre*: The Vocation of Memory and the Space of Writing.' *Research in African Literatures*, 29:2 (1998 Summer), 76–93.

Ka, Aminata Maiga. 'Ramatoulaye, Aissatou, Mireille, et ... Mariama Bâ.' *Notre Librairie*, 81 (1985), 129–34.

Kempen, Laura Charlotte. *Mariama Bâ, Rigoberta Menchú, and Postcolonial Feminism*. New York: P. Lang, 2001.

King, Adele. 'The Personal and the Political in the Work of Mariama Bâ.' *Studies in Twentieth Century Literature*, 18.2 (1994), 177–88.

Makward, Edris. 'Marriage, Tradition and Woman's Pursuit of Happiness in the Novels of Mariama Bâ.' *Ngambika: Studies of Women in African Literature*. Ed: Carole Boyce Davies and Anne Adams Graves. Trenton, NJ: Africa World Press, 1986. 241–56.

McElaney-Johnson, Ann. 'Epistolary Friendship: La Prise de parole in Mariama Bâ's *Une si longue lettre*.' *Research in African Literatures*, 30:2 (1999 Summer), 110–21.

Miller, Christopher L. *Theories of Africans*. Chicago: University of Chicago Press, 1990.

Mortimer, Mildred. *Journeys Through the French African Novel*. Portsmouth, NH: Heinemann, 1990.

Nnaemeka, Obioma. 'Mariama Ba: Parallels, Convergence and Interior Space.' *Feminist Issues*, 10.1 (1990), 13–35.

Ojo-Ade, Femi. 'Still a Victim? Mariama Bâ's *Une si longue lettre*.' *African Literature Today*, 12 (1982), 71–87.

Pritchett, James A. 'Mariama Bâ's *So Long a Letter.*' In Hay, Margaret Jean (ed. and introd.), *African Novels in the Classroom.* Boulder, Colorado: Rienner, 2000.

Reyes, Angelita. 'The Epistolary Voice and Voices of Indigenous Feminism in Mariama Bâ's *Une si longue lettre.*' In Davies, Carole Boyce (ed. and introd.), *Moving beyond Boundaries II: Black Women's Diasporas.* New York, NY: New York University Press, 1994.

Sarvan, Charles Ponnuthurai. 'Feminism and African Fiction: The Novels of Mariama Bâ.' *Modern Fiction Studies*, 34.3 (1988), 453–64.

To Abibatou Niang, pure and constant,
lucid and thorough, who shares my feelings.

To Annette d'Erneville of the warm heart and level head.

To all women and to men of good will.

Dear Aissatou,

I have received your letter. By way of reply, I am beginning this diary, my prop in my distress. Our long association has taught me that confiding in others allays pain.

Your presence in my life is by no means fortuitous. Our grandmothers in their compounds were separated by a fence and would exchange messages daily. Our mothers used to argue over who would look after our uncles and aunts. As for us, we wore out wrappers and sandals on the same stony road to the koranic school; we buried our milk teeth in the same holes and begged our fairy godmothers to restore them to us, more splendid than before.

If over the years, and passing through the realities of life, dreams die, I still keep intact my memories, the salt of remembrance.

I conjure you up. The past is reborn, along with its procession of emotions. I close my eyes. Ebb and tide of feeling: heat and dazzlement, the woodfires, the sharp green mango, bitten into in turns, a delicacy in our greedy mouths. I close my eyes. Ebb and tide of images: drops of sweat beading your mother's ochre-coloured face as she emerges from the kitchen; the procession of young wet girls chattering on their way back from the springs.

We walked the same paths from adolescence to maturity, where the past begets the present.

My friend, my friend, my friend. I call on you three times.[1*]
Yesterday you were divorced. Today I am a widow.

Modou is dead. How am I to tell you? One does not fix appointments with fate. Fate grasps whom it wants, when it wants. When it moves in the direction of your desires, it brings you

* Notes are to be found on p.96.

plenitude. But more often than not, it unsettles, crosses you. Then one has to endure. I endured the telephone call which disrupted my life.

A taxi quickly hailed! Fast! Fast! Faster still! My throat is dry. There is a rigid lump in my chest. Fast: faster still. At last, the hospital: the mixed smell of suppurations and ether. The hospital – distorted faces, a train of tearful people, known and unknown, witnesses to this awful tragedy. A long corridor, which seems to stretch out endlessly. At the end, a room. In the room, a bed. On the bed, Modou stretched out, cut off from the world of the living by a white sheet in which he is completely enveloped. A trembling hand moves forward and slowly uncovers the body. His hairy chest, at rest forever, is visible through his crumpled blue shirt with thin stripes. This face, set in pain and surprise, is indeed his, the bald forehead, the half-open mouth are indeed his. I want to grasp his hand. But someone pulls me away. I can hear Mawdo, his doctor friend, explaining to me: a heart attack came on suddenly in his office while he was dictating a letter. The secretary had the presence of mind to call me. Mawdo recounts how he arrived too late with the ambulance. I think: the doctor after death. He mimes the massaging of the heart that was undertaken, as well as the futile effort at mouth-to-mouth resuscitation. Again, I think: heart massage, mouth-to-mouth resuscitation, ridiculous weapons against the divine will.

I listen to the words that create around me a new atmosphere in which I move, a stranger and tormented. Death, the tenuous passage between two opposite worlds, one tumultuous, the other still.

Where to lie down? Middle age demands dignity. I hold tightly on to my prayer beads. I tell the beads ardently, remaining standing on legs of jelly. My loins beat as to the rhythm of childbirth.

Cross-sections of my life spring involuntarily from my memory, grandiose verses from the Koran, noble words of consolation fight for my attention.

Joyous miracle of birth, dark miracle of death. Between the two, a life, a destiny, says Mawdo Bâ.

I look intently at Mawdo. He seems to be taller than usual in his white overall. He seems to me thin. His reddened eyes express forty years of friendship. I admire his noble hands, hands of an absolute delicacy, supple hands used to tracking down illness. Those hands, moved by friendship and a rigorous science, could not save his friend.

2

Modou Fall is indeed dead, Aissatou. The uninterrupted procession of men and women who have 'learned' of it, the wails and tears all around me, confirm his death. This condition of extreme tension sharpens my suffering and continues till the following day, the day of interment.

What a seething crowd of human beings come from all parts of the country, where the radio has relayed the news.

Women, close relatives, are busy. They must take incense, eau-de-cologne, cotton-wool to the hospital for the washing of the dead one. The seven metres of white muslin, the only clothing Islam allows for the dead, are carefully placed in a new basket. The *Zem-Zem*, the miracle water from the holy places of Islam religiously kept by each family, is not forgotten. Rich, dark wrappers are chosen to cover Modou.

My back propped up by cushions, legs outstretched, my head covered with a black wrapper, I follow the comings and goings of people. Across from me, a new winnowing fan bought for the occasion receives the first alms. The presence of my co-wife beside me irritates me. She has been installed in my house for the funeral, in accordance with tradition. With each passing hour her cheeks become more deeply hollowed, acquire ever more rings, those big and beautiful eyes which open and close on their secrets, perhaps their regrets. At the age of love and freedom from care, this child is dogged by sadness.

While the men, in a long, irregular file of official and private cars, public buses, lorries and mopeds, accompany Modou to his last rest (people were for a long time to talk of the crowd which followed the funeral procession), our sisters-in-law undo our hair. My co-wife and myself are put inside a rough and ready tent made of a wrapper pulled taut above our heads and set up for the occasion. While our sisters-in-law are constructing it, the women present, informed of the work in hand, get up and throw some coins onto the fluttering canopy so as to ward off evil spirits.

This is the moment dreaded by every Senegalese woman, the moment when she sacrifices her possessions as gifts to her family-in-law; and, worse still, beyond her possessions she gives up her personality, her dignity, becoming a thing in the service of the man who has married her, his grandfather, his grandmother, his father, his mother, his brother, his sister, his uncle, his aunt, his male and female cousins, his friends. Her behaviour is conditioned: no sister-in-law will touch the head of any wife who has been stingy, unfaithful or inhospitable.

As for ourselves, we have been deserving, and our sisters-in-law sing a chorus of praises chanted at the top of their voices. Our patience before all trials, the frequency of our gifts find their justification and reward today. Our sisters-in-law give equal consideration to thirty years and five years of married life. With the same ease and the same words, they celebrate twelve maternities and three. I note with outrage this desire to level out, in which Modou's new mother-in-law rejoices.

4

Having washed their hands in a bowl of water placed at the entrance to the house, the men, back from the cemetery, file past the family grouped around us, the widows. They offer their condolences punctuated with praises of the deceased.

'Modou, friend of the young as of the old ...'

'Modou, the lion-hearted, champion of the oppressed ...'

'Modou, at ease as much in a suit as in a caftan ...'

'Modou, good brother, good husband, good Muslim ...'

'May God forgive him ...'

'May he regret his earthly stay in his heavenly bliss ...'

'May the earth rest lightly on him!'

They are there, his childhood playmates on the football ground, or during bird hunts, when they used catapults. They are there, his classmates. They are there, his companions in the trade union struggles.

The *Siguil ndigale*[2] come one after the other, poignant, while skilled hands distribute to the crowd biscuits, sweets, cola nuts, judiciously mixed, the first offerings to heaven for the peaceful repose of the deceased's soul.

3

On the third day, the same comings and goings of friends, relatives, the poor, the unknown. The name of the deceased, who was popular, has mobilized a buzzing crowd, welcomed in my house that has been stripped of all that could be stolen, all that could be spoilt. Mats of all sorts are spread out everywhere there is space. Metal chairs hired for the occasion take on a blue hue in the sun.

Comforting words from the Koran fill the air; divine words, divine instructions, impressive promises of punishment or joy, exhortations to virtue, warnings against evil, exaltation of humility, of faith. Shivers run through me. My tears flow and my voice joins weakly in the fervent 'Amen' which inspires the crowd's ardour at the end of each verse.

The smell of the *lakh*[3] cooling in the calabashes pervades the air, exciting.

Also passed around are large bowls of red or white rice, cooked here or in neighbouring houses. Iced fruit juices, water and curds are served in plastic cups. The men's group eats in silence. Perhaps they remember the stiff body, tied up and lowered by their hands into a gaping hole, quickly covered up again.

In the women's corner, nothing but noise, resonant laughter, loud talk, hand slaps, strident exclamations. Friends who have not seen each other for a long time hug each other noisily. Some discuss the latest material on the market. Others indicate where they got their woven wrappers from. The latest bits of gossip are exchanged. They laugh heartily and roll their eyes and admire the next person's *boubou*, her original way of using henna to blacken hands and feet by drawing geometrical figures on them.

From time to time an exasperated manly voice rings out a warning, recalls the purpose of the gathering: a ceremony for the redemption of a soul. The voice is quickly forgotten and the brou-haha begins all over again, increasing in volume.

In the evening comes the most disconcerting part of this third day's ceremony. More people, more jostling in order to hear and see better. Groups are formed according to relationships, according to blood ties, areas, corporations. Each group displays its own contribution to the costs. In former times this contribution was made in kind: millet, livestock, rice, flour, oil, sugar, milk. Today it is made conspicuously in banknotes, and no one wants to give less than the other. A disturbing display of inner feeling that cannot be evaluated now measured in francs! And again I think how many of the dead would have survived if, before organizing these festive funeral ceremonies, the relative or friend had bought the life-saving prescription or paid for hospitalization.

The takings are carefully recorded. It is a debt to be repaid in similar circumstances. Modou's relatives open an exercise book. Lady Mother-in-Law (Modou's) and her daughter have a notebook. Fatimi, my younger sister, carefully records my takings in a note-pad.

As I come from a large family in this town, with acquaintances at all levels of society, as I am a schoolteacher on friendly terms with the pupils' parents, and as I have been Modou's companion for thirty years, I receive the greater share of money and many envelopes. The regard shown me raises me in the eyes of the others and it is Lady Mother-in-Law's turn to be annoyed. Newly admitted into the city's bourgeoisie by her daughter's marriage, she too reaps banknotes. As for her silent, haggard child, she remains a stranger in these circles.

The sudden calls from our sisters-in-law bring her out of her stupor. They reappear after their deliberation. They have contributed the large sum of two hundred thousand francs to 'dress' us.[4] Yesterday, they offered us some excellent *thiakry*[5] to quench our thirst. The Fall family's *griot*[6] is proud of her role as go-between, a role handed down from mother to daughter.

'One hundred thousand francs from the father's side.'

'One hundred thousand francs from the mother's side.'

She counts the notes, blue and pink, one by one, shows them round and concludes: 'I have much to say about you Falls, grandchildren of Damel Madiodio, who have inherited royal blood. But one of you is no more. Today is not a happy day. I weep with you for Modou, whom I used to call "bag of rice", for he would frequently give me a sack of rice. Therefore accept this money, you worthy widows of a worthy man.'

The share of each widow must be doubled, as must the gifts of Modou's grandchildren, represented by the offspring of all his male and female cousins.

Thus our family-in-law take away with them a wad of notes, painstakingly topped, and leave us utterly destitute, we who will need material support.

Afterwards comes the procession of old relatives, old acquaintances, *griots*, goldsmiths, *laobés* with their honeyed language. The 'goodbyes' following one after the other at an infernal rate are irritating because they are neither simple nor free: they require, depending on the person leaving, sometimes a coin, sometimes a banknote.

Gradually the house empties. The smells of stale sweat and food blend as trails in the air, unpleasant and nauseating. Cola nuts spat out here and there have left red stains: my tiles, kept with such painstaking care, are blackened. Oil stains on the walls, balls of crumpled paper. What a balance sheet for a day!

My horizon lightened, I see an old woman. Who is she? Where is she from? Bent over, the ends of her *boubou* tied behind her, she empties into a plastic bag the left-overs of red rice. Her smiling face tells of the pleasant day she has just had. She wants to take back proof of this to her family, living perhaps in Ouakam, Thiaroye or Pikine.[7]

Standing upright, her eyes meeting my disapproving look, she mutters between teeth reddened by cola nuts: 'Lady, death is just as beautiful as life has been.'

◊

Alas, it's the same story on the eighth and fortieth days, when those who have 'learned' belatedly make up for lost time. Light attire showing off slim waistlines, prominent backsides, the new brassiere or the one bought at the second-hand market, chewing sticks wedged between teeth, white or flowered shawls, heavy smell of incense and of *gongo*[8], loud voices, strident laughter. And yet we are told in the Koran that on the third day the dead body swells and fills its tomb; we are told that on the eighth it bursts; and we are also told that on the fortieth day it is stripped. What then is the significance of these joyous, institutionalized festivities that accompany our prayers for God's mercy? Who has come out of self-interest? Who has come to quench his own thirst? Who has come for the sake of mercy? Who has come so that he may remember?

Tonight Binetou, my co-wife, will return to her SICAP[9] villa. At last! Phew!

The visits of condolence continue: the sick, those who have journeyed or have merely arrived late, as well as the lazy, come to fulfil what they consider to be a sacred duty. Child-naming ceremonies may be missed but never a funeral. Coins and notes continue to pour on the beckoning fan.

Alone, I live in a monotony broken only by purifying baths, the changing of my mourning clothes every Monday and Friday.

I hope to carry out my duties fully. My heart concurs with the demands of religion. Reared since childhood on their strict precepts, I expect not to fail. The walls that limit my horizon for four months and ten days do not bother me. I have enough memories in me to ruminate upon. And these are what I am afraid of, for they smack of bitterness.

May their evocation not soil the state of purity in which I must live.

Till tomorrow.

4

Aissatou, my friend, perhaps I am boring you by relating what you already know.

I have never observed so much, because I have never been so concerned.

The family meeting held this morning in my sitting-room is at last over. You can easily guess those who were present: Lady Mother-in-Law, her brother and her daughter, Binetou, who is even thinner; old Tamsir, Modou's brother, and the *Imam* from the mosque in his area; Mawdo Bâ; my daughter and her husband Abdou.

The *mirasse* commanded by the Koran requires that a dead person be stripped of his most intimate secrets; thus is exposed to others what was carefully concealed. These exposures crudely explain a man's life. With consternation, I measure the extent of Modou's betrayal. His abandonment of his first family (myself and my children) was the outcome of the choice of a new life. He rejected us. He mapped out his future without taking our existence into account.

His promotion to the rank of technical adviser in the Ministry of Public Works, in exchange for which, according to the spiteful, he checked the trade union revolt, could not control the mire of expenses by which he was engulfed. Dead without a penny saved. Acknowledgement of debts? A pile of them: cloth and gold traders, home-delivery grocers and butchers, car-purchase instalments.

Hold on. The star attraction of this 'stripping': the origins of the elegant SICAP villa, four bedrooms, two bathrooms, pink and blue, large sitting-room, a three-room flat, built at his own expense at the bottom of the second courtyard for Lady Mother-in-Law. And furniture from France for his new wife and furniture constructed by local carpenters for Lady Mother-in-Law.

This house and its chic contents were acquired by a bank loan granted on the mortgage of 'Villa Fallene', where I live. Although the title deeds of this house bear his name, it is nonetheless our common property, acquired by our joint savings. Insult upon injury!

Moreover, he continued the monthly payments of seventy-five thousand francs to the SICAP. These payments were to go on for about ten years before the house would become his.

Four million francs borrowed with ease because of his privileged position, which had enabled him to pay for Lady Mother-in-Law and her husband to visit Mecca to acquire the titles of *Alhaja* and *Alhaji*; which equally enabled Binetou to exchange her Alfa Romeos at the slightest dent.

Now I understand the terrible significance of Modou's abandonment of our joint bank account. He wanted to be financially independent so as to have enough elbow room.

And then, having withdrawn Binetou from school, he paid her a monthly allowance of fifty thousand francs, just like a salary due to her. The young girl, who was very gifted, wanted to continue her studies, to sit for her *baccalauréat*. So as to establish his rule, Modou, wickedly, determined to remove her from the critical and unsparing world of the young. He therefore gave in to all the conditions of the grasping Lady Mother-in-Law and even signed a paper committing himself to paying the said amount. Lady Mother-in-Law brandished the paper, for she firmly believed that the payments would continue, even after Modou's death, out of the estate.

As for my daughter, Daba, she waved about a bailiff's affidavit, dated the very day of her father's death, that listed all the contents of the SICAP villa. The list supplied by Lady Mother-in-Law and Binetou made no mention of certain objects and items of furniture, which had mysteriously disappeared or had been fraudulently removed.

You know that I am excessively sentimental. I was not at all pleased by this display on either side.

5

When I stopped yesterday, I probably left you astonished by my disclosures.

Was it madness, weakness, irresistible love? What inner confusion led Modou Fall to marry Binetou?

To overcome my bitterness, I think of human destiny. Each life has its share of heroism, an obscure heroism, born of abdication, of renunciation and acceptance under the merciless whip of fate.

I think of all the blind people the world over, moving in darkness. I think of all the paralysed the world over, dragging themselves about. I think of all the lepers the world over, wasted by their disease.

Victims of a sad fate which you did not choose, compared with your lamentations, what is my quarrel, cruelly motivated, with a dead man who no longer has any hold over my destiny? Combining your despair, you could have been avengers and made them tremble, all those who are drunk on their wealth; tremble, those upon whom fate has bestowed favours. A horde powerful in its repugnance and revolt, you could have snatched the bread that your hunger craves.

Your stoicism has made you not violent or subversive but true heroes, unknown in the mainstream of history, never upsetting established order, despite your miserable condition.

I repeat, beside your visible deformities, what are moral infirmities from which in any case you are not immune? Thinking of you, I thank God for my eyes which daily embrace heaven and earth. If today moral fatigue makes my limbs stiff, tomorrow it will leave my body. Then, relieved, my legs will carry me slowly and I shall again have around me the iodine and the blue of the sea. The star and white cloud will be mine. The breath of wind will again refresh my face. I will stretch out, turn around, I will vibrate. Oh, health, live in me. Oh, health ...

My efforts cannot for long take my mind off my disappointment. I think of the suckling baby, no sooner born than orphaned. I think of the blind man who will never see his child's smile. I think of the cross the one-armed man has to bear. I think ... But my despair persists, but my rancour remains, but the waves of an immense sadness break in me!

Madness or weakness? Heartlessness or irresistible love? What inner torment led Modou Fall to marry Binetou?

And to think that I loved this man passionately, to think that I gave him thirty years of my life, to think that twelve times over I carried his child. The addition of a rival to my life was not enough for him. In loving someone else, he burned his past, both morally and materially. He dared to commit such an act of disavowal.

And yet, what didn't he do to make me his wife!

6

Do you remember the morning train that took us for the first time to Ponty-Ville, the teachers' training college in Sebikotane? Ponty-Ville is the countryside still green from the last rains, a celebration of youth right in the middle of nature, banjo music in dormitories transformed into dance floors, conversations held along the rows of geraniums or under the thick mango trees.

Modou Fall, the very moment you bowed before me, asking me to dance, I knew you were the one I was waiting for. Tall and athletically built, of course. Olive-coloured skin due to your distant Moorish blood, no question. Virility and fineness of features harmoniously blended, once again, no question. But, above all, you knew how to be tender. You could fathom every thought, every desire. You knew many undefinable things, which glorified you and sealed our relationship.

As we danced, your forehead, hairline already receding, bent over my own. The same happy smile lit up our faces. The pressure of your hand became more tender, more possessive. Everything in me gave in and our relationship endured over the school years and during the holidays, strengthened in me by the discovery of your subtle intelligence, of your embracing sensitivity, of your readiness to help, of your ambition, which suffered no mediocrity. It was this ambition which led you, on leaving school, to prepare on your own for the two examinations of the *baccalauréat*. Then you left for France and, according to your letters, you lived there as a recluse, attaching little importance to the glitter that met your regard; but you grasped the deep sense of a history that has worked so many wonders and of a great culture that overwhelmed you. The milky complexion of the women had no hold on you. Again, quoting from your letters: 'On the strictly physical plane, the white woman's advantage over the black woman lies in the variety of her colour, the abundance, length and softness of her hair. There are also the eyes which can be blue, green, often the colour of new honey.' You also used to complain of the sombreness of the skies, under which no coconut trees waved their tops. You missed the swinging hips of black women walking along the pavements, this gracious deliberate slowness characteristic of Africa, which charmed your eyes. You were sick at heart at the dogged rhythm of the life of the people and the numbing effect of the cold. You would finish by saying that your studies were your staff, your buttress. You would end with a string of endearments and conclude by reassuring me: 'It's you whom I carry within me. You are my protecting black angel. Would I could quickly find you, if only to hold your hand tightly so that I may forget hunger and thirst and loneliness.'

And you returned in triumph. With a degree in law! In spite of your voice and your gift of oratory, you preferred obscure work,

14

less well paid but constructive for your country, to the showiness of the lawyer.

Your achievement did not stop there. Your introduction of your friend Mawdo Bâ into our circle was to change the life of my best friend, Aissatou.

I no longer scorn my mother's reserve concerning you, for a mother can instinctively feel where her child's happiness lies. I no longer laugh when I think that she found you too handsome, too polished, too perfect for a man. She often spoke of the wide gap between your two upper incisors: the sign of the primacy of sensuality in the individual. What didn't she do, from then on, to separate us? She could see in you only the eternal khaki suit, the uniform of your school. All she remembered of you were your visits, considered too long. You were idle, she said, therefore with plenty of time to waste. And you would use that time to 'stuff' my head, to the disadvantage of more interesting young people.

Because, being the first pioneers of the promotion of African women, there were very few of us. Men would call us scatter-brained. Others labelled us devils. But many wanted to possess us. How many dreams did we nourish hopelessly that could have been fulfilled as lasting happiness and that we abandoned to embrace others, those that have burst miserably like soap bubbles, leaving us empty-handed?

7

Aissatou, I will never forget the white woman who was the first to desire for us an 'uncommon' destiny. Together, let us recall our school, green, pink, blue, yellow, a veritable rainbow: green, blue and yellow, the colours of the flowers everywhere in the compound; pink the colour of the dormitories, with the beds

15

impeccably made. Let us hear the walls of our school come to life with the intensity of our study. Let us relive its intoxicating atmosphere at night, while the evening song, our joint prayer, rang out, full of hope. The admission policy, which was based on an entrance examination for the whole of former French West Africa, now broken up into autonomous republics, made possible a fruitful blend of different intellects, characters, manners and customs. Nothing differentiated us, apart from specific racial features, the Fon girl from Dahomey and the Malinke one from Guinea. Friendships were made that have endured the test of time and distance. We were true sisters, destined for the same mission of emancipation.

To lift us out of the bog of tradition, superstition and custom, to make us appreciate a multitude of civilizations without renouncing our own, to raise our vision of the world, cultivate our personalities, strengthen our qualities, to make up for our inadequacies, to develop universal moral values in us: these were the aims of our admirable headmistress. The word 'love' had a particular resonance in her. She loved us without patronizing us, with our plaits either standing on end or bent down, with our loose blouses, our wrappers. She knew how to discover and appreciate our qualities.

How I think of her! If the memory of her has triumphed over the ingratitude of time, now that flowers no longer smell as sweetly or as strongly as before, now that age and mature reflection have stripped our dreams of their poetic virtue, it is because the path chosen for our training and our blossoming has not been at all fortuitous. It has accorded with the profound choices made by New Africa for the promotion of the black woman.

Thus, free from frustrating taboos and capable now of discernment, why should I follow my mother's finger pointing at Daouda Dieng, still a bachelor but too mature for my eighteen years? Working as an African doctor at the Polyclinique, he was well-to-do and knew how to use his position to advantage. His villa, perched on a rock on the Corniche facing the sea, was the meeting place for the young elite. Nothing was missing, from the refrigerator, containing its pleasant drinks, to the record player, which exuded sometimes languorous, sometimes frenzied music.

Daouda Dieng also knew how to win hearts. Useful presents for my mother, ranging from a sack of rice, appreciated in that period of war penury, to the frivolous gift for me, daintily wrapped in paper and tied with ribbons. But I preferred the man in the eternal khaki suit. Our marriage was celebrated without dowry, without pomp, under the disapproving looks of my father, before the painful indignation of my frustrated mother, under the sarcasm of my surprised sisters, in our town struck dumb with astonishment.

8

Then came your marriage with Mawdo Bâ, recently graduated from the African School of Medicine and Pharmacy. A controversial marriage. I can still hear the angry rumours in town:

'What, a Toucouleur marrying a goldsmith's daughter? He will never "make money".'

'Mawdo's mother is a Dioufene, a *Guelewar*[10] from the Sine. What an insult to her, before her former co-wives.' (Mawdo's father was dead.)

'In the desire to marry a "short skirt" come what may, this is what one gets.'

'School turns our girls into devils who lure our men away from the right path.'

And I haven't recounted all. But Mawdo remained firm. 'Marriage is a personal thing,' he retorted to anyone who cared to hear.

He emphasized his total commitment to his choice of life

partner by visiting your father, not at home but at his place of work. He would return from his outings illuminated, happy to have 'moved in the right direction,' he would say triumphantly. He would speak of your father as a 'creative artist'. He admired the man, weakened as he was by the daily dose of carbon dioxide he inhaled working in the acrid atmosphere of the dusty fumes. Gold is his medium, which he melts, pours, twists, flattens, refines, chases. 'You should see him,' Mawdo would add. 'You should see him breathe over the flame.' His cheeks would swell with the life from his lungs. This life would animate the flame, sometimes red, sometimes blue, which would rise or curve, wax or wane at his command, depending on what the work demanded. And the gold specks in the showers of red sparks, and the uncouth songs of the apprentices punctuating the strokes of the hammer here, and the pressure of hands on the bellows there, would make passers-by turn round.

Aissatou, your father knew all the rites that protect the working of gold, the metal of the djinns. Each profession has its code, known only to the initiated and transmitted from father to son. As soon as your elder brothers left the huts of the circumcised, they moved into this particular world, the whole compound's source of nourishment.

But what about your younger brothers? Their steps were directed towards the white man's school. Hard is the climb up the steep hill of knowledge to the white man's school: kindergarten remains a luxury that only those who are financially sound can offer their young ones. Yet it is necessary, for this is what sharpens and channels the young ones' attention and sensibilities.

Even though the primary schools are rapidly increasing, access to them has not become any easier. They leave out in the streets an impressive number of children because of the lack of places.

Entrance into secondary school is no panacea for the child at an age fraught with the problems of consolidating his personality, with the explosion of puberty, with the discovery of the various pitfalls: drugs, vagrancy, sensuality.

The university has its own large number of despairing rejects.

What will the unsuccessful do? Apprenticeship to traditional crafts seems degrading to whoever has the slightest book-learning. The dream is to become a clerk. The trowel is spurned.

The horde of the jobless swells the flood of delinquency.

Should we have been happy at the desertion of the forges, the workshops, the shoemakers' shops? Should we have rejoiced so wholeheartedly? Were we not beginning to witness the disappearance of an elite of traditional manual workers?

Eternal questions of our eternal debates. We all agreed that much dismantling was needed to introduce modernity within our traditions. Torn between the past and the present, we deplored the 'hard sweat' that would be inevitable. We counted the possible losses. But we knew that nothing would be as before. We were full of nostalgia but were resolutely progressive.

9

Mawdo raised you up to his own level, he the son of a princess and you a child from the forges. His mother's rejection did not frighten him.

Our lives developed in parallel. We experienced the tiffs and reconciliations of married life. In our different ways, we suffered the social constraints and heavy burden of custom. I loved Modou. I compromised with his people. I tolerated his sisters, who too often would desert their own homes to encumber my own. They allowed themselves to be fed and petted. They would look on, without reacting, as their children romped around on my chairs. I tolerated their spitting, the phlegm expertly secreted under my carpets.

His mother would stop by again and again while on her outings, always flanked by different friends, just to show off her son's social success but particularly so that they might see, at close quarters, her supremacy in this beautiful house in which she did not live. I would receive her with all the respect due to a queen, and she would leave satisfied, especially if her hand closed over the banknote I had carefully placed there. But hardly would she be out than she would think of the new band of friends she would soon be dazzling.

Modou's father was more understanding. More often than not, he would visit us without sitting down. He would accept a glass of cold water and would leave, after repeating his prayers for the protection of the house.

I knew how to smile at them all, and consented to wasting useful time in futile chatter. My sisters-in-law believed me to be spared the drudgery of housework.

'With your two housemaids!' they would say with emphasis.

Try explaining to them that a working woman is no less responsible for her home. Try explaining to them that nothing is done if you do not step in, that you have to see to everything, do everything all over again: cleaning up, cooking, ironing. There are the children to be washed, the husband to be looked after. The working woman has a dual task, of which both halves, equally arduous, must be reconciled. How does one go about this? Therein lies the skill that makes all the difference to a home.

Some of my sisters-in-law did not envy my way of living at all. They saw me dashing around the house after a hard day at school. They appreciated their comfort, their peace of mind, their moments of leisure and allowed themselves to be looked after by their husbands, who were crushed under their duties.

Others, limited in their way of thinking, envied my comfort and purchasing power. They would go into raptures over the many 'gadgets' in my house: gas cooker, vegetable grater, sugar tongs. They forgot the source of this easy life; first up in the morning, last to go to bed, always working.

You, Aissatou, you forsook your family-in-law, tightly shut in with their hurt dignity. You would lament to me: 'Your family-in-law respects you. You must treat them well. As for me, they look down on me from the height of their lost nobility. What can I do?'

While Mawdo's mother planned her revenge, we lived: Christmas Eve parties organized by several couples, with the costs shared equally, and held in turns in the different homes. Without self-consciousness, we would revive the dances of yester-year: the lively beguine, frenzied rumbas, languid tangos. We rediscovered the old beatings of the heart that strengthened our feelings.

We would also leave the stifling city to breathe in the healthy air of seaside suburbs.

We would walk along the Dakar Corniche, one of the most beautiful in West Africa, a sheer work of art wrought by nature. Rounded or pointed rocks, black or ochre-coloured, overlooking the ocean. Greenery, sometimes a veritable hanging garden, spread out under the clear sky. We would go on to the road to Ouakam, which also leads to Ngor and further on to Yoff Airport. We would recognize on the way the narrow road leading farther on to Almadies beach.

Our favourite spot was Ngor beach, situated near the village of the same name, where old bearded fishermen repaired their nets under the silk-cotton trees. Naked and snotty children played in complete freedom when they were not frolicking about in the sea.

On the fine sand, washed by the waves and swollen with water, naively painted canoes awaited their turn to be launched into the waters. In their hollows small pools of blue water would glisten, full of light from the sky and sun.

What a crowd on public holidays! Numerous families would stroll about, thirsty for space and fresh air. People would undress, without embarrassment, tempted by the benevolent caress of the iodized breeze and the warmth from the sun's rays. The idle would sleep under spread parasols. A few children, spade and bucket in hand, would build and demolish the castles of their imagination.

In the evening the fishermen would return from their laborious outings. Once more, they had escaped the moving snare of the sea. At first simple points on the horizon, the boats would become more distinct from one another as they drew nearer. They would dance in the hollows of the waves, then would lazily let themselves be dragged along. Fishermen would gaily furl their sails and draw in their tackle. While some of them would gather together the wriggling catch, others would wring out their soaked clothes and mop their faces.

Under the wondering gaze of the kids, the live fish would flip up as the long sea snakes would curve themselves inwards. There is nothing more beautiful than a fish just out of water, its eye clear and fresh, with golden or silvery scales and beautiful blueish glints!

Hands would sort out, group, divide. We would buy a good selection at bargain prices for the house.

The sea air would put us in good humour. The pleasure we indulged in and in which all our senses rejoiced would intoxicate both rich and poor with health. Our communion with deep, bottomless and unlimited nature refreshed our souls. Depression and sadness would disappear, suddenly to be replaced by feelings of plenitude and expansiveness.

Reinvigorated, we would set out for home. How jealously we guarded the secret of simple pleasures, health-giving remedy for the daily tensions of life.

Do you remember the picnics we organized at Sangalkam, in the farm Mawdo Bâ inherited from his father? Sangalkam remains the refuge of people from Dakar, those who want a break from the frenzy of the city. The younger set, in particular, has bought land there and built country residences: these green, open spaces are conducive to rest, meditation and the letting off of steam by children. This oasis lies on the road to Rufisque.

Mawdo's mother had looked after the farm before her son's marriage. The memory of her husband had made her attached to this plot of land, where their joint and patient hands had disciplined the vegetation that filled our eyes with admiration.

Yourself, you added the small building at the far end: three small, simple bedrooms, a bathroom, a kitchen. You grew many flowers in a few corners. You had a hen run built, then a closed pen for sheep.

Coconut trees, with their interlacing leaves, gave protection from the sun. Succulent sapodilla stood next to sweet-smelling pomegranates. Heavy mangoes weighed down the branches. Pawpaws resembling breasts of different shapes hung tempting and inaccessible from the tops of elongated trunks.

Green leaves and browned leaves, new grass and withered grass were strewn all over the ground. Under our feet the ants untiringly built and rebuilt their homes.

How warm the shades over the camp beds! Teams for games were formed one after the other amid cries of victory or lamentations of defeat.

And we stuffed ourselves with fruits within easy reach. And we drank the milk from coconuts. And we told 'juicy stories'! And we danced about, roused by the strident notes of a gramophone. And the lamb, seasoned with white pepper, garlic, butter, hot pepper, would be roasting over the wood fire.

And we lived. When we stood in front of our over-crowded classes, we represented a force in the enormous effort to be accomplished in order to overcome ignorance.

Each profession, intellectual or manual, deserves consideration, whether it requires painful physical effort or manual dexterity, wide knowledge or the patience of an ant. Ours, like that of the doctor, does not allow for any mistake. You don't joke with life, and life is both body and mind. To warp a soul is as much a sacrilege as murder. Teachers – at kindergarten level, as at university level – form a noble army accomplishing daily feats, never praised, never decorated. An army forever on the move, forever vigilant. An army without drums, without gleaming uniforms. This army, thwarting traps and snares, everywhere plants the flag of knowledge and morality.

How we loved this priesthood, humble teachers in humble local schools. How faithfully we served our profession, and how we spent ourselves in order to do it honour. Like all apprentices, we had learned how to practise it well at the demonstration school, a few steps away from our own, where experienced teachers taught the novices that we were how to apply, in the lessons we gave, our knowledge of psychology and method ... In those children we set in motion waves that, breaking, carried away in their furl a bit of ourselves.

10

Modou rose steadily to the top rank in the trade union organizations. His understanding of people and things endeared him to both employers and workers. He focused his efforts on points that were easily satisfied, that made work lighter and life more pleasant. He sought practical improvements in the workers' conditions. His slogan was: what's the use of taunting with the impossible? Obtaining the 'possible' is already a victory.

His point of view was not unanimously accepted, but people relied on his practical realism.

Mawdo could take part in neither trade unionism nor politics, for he hadn't the time. His reputation as a good doctor was growing; he remained the prisoner of his mission in a hospital filled to capacity with the sick, for people were going less and less to the native doctor who specialized in brewing the same concoctions of leaves for different illnesses.

Everybody was reading newspapers and magazines. There was unrest in North Africa.

Did these interminable discussions, during which points of view concurred or clashed, complemented each other or were vanquished, determine the aspect of the New Africa?

The assimilationist dream of the colonist drew into its crucible our mode of thought and way of life. The sun helmet worn over the natural protection of our kinky hair, smoke-filled pipe in the mouth, white shorts just above the calves, very short dresses displaying shapely legs: a whole generation suddenly became aware of the ridiculous situation festering in our midst.

History marched on, inexorably. The debate over the right path to take shook West Africa. Brave men went to prison; others, following in their footsteps, continued the work begun.

It was the privilege of our generation to be the link between two periods in our history, one of domination, the other of independence. We remained young and efficient, for we were the messengers of a new design. With independence achieved, we witnessed the birth of a republic, the birth of an anthem and the implantation of a flag.

I heard people repeat that all the active forces in the country should be mobilized. And we said that over and above the unavoidable opting for such-and-such a party, such-and-such a model of society, what was needed was national unity. Many of us rallied around the dominant party, infusing it with new blood. To be productive in the crowd was better than crossing one's arms and hiding behind imported ideologies.

Modou, a practical man, led his unions into collaboration with the government, demanding for his troops only what was possible. But he cursed the hasty establishment of too many embassies, which he judged to be too costly for our under-developed country. This bleeding of the country for reasons of pure vanity, among other things, such as the frequent invitation of foreigners, was just a waste of money. And, with his wage-earners in mind, he would repeatedly growl, 'So many schools, or so much hospital equipment lost! So many monthly wage increases! So many tarred roads!'

You and Mawdo would listen to him. We were scaling the heights, but your mother-in-law, who saw you resplendent beside her son, who saw her son going more and more frequently to your father's workshop, who saw your mother fill out and dress better, your mother-in-law thought more and more of her revenge.

11

I know that I am shaking you, that I am twisting a knife in a wound hardly healed; but what can I do? I cannot help remembering in my forced solitude and reclusion.

Mawdo's mother is Aunty Nabou to us and Seynabou to others. She bore a glorious name in the Sine: Diouf. She is a descendant of Bour-Sine. She lived in the past, unaware of the changing world. She clung to old beliefs. Being strongly attached to her privileged origins, she believed firmly that blood carried with it virtues, and, nodding her head, she would repeat that humble birth would always show in a person's bearing. And life had not been kind to Mawdo's mother. Very early, she lost her dear husband; bravely, she brought up her eldest son Mawdo and two other daughters, now married ... and well married. She devoted herself

26

with the affection of a tigress to her 'one and only man', Mawdo Bâ. When she swore by her only son's nose, the symbol of life, she had said everything. Now, her 'only man' was moving away from her, through the fault of this cursed daughter of a goldsmith, worse than a *griot* woman. The *griot* brings happiness. But a goldsmith's daughter! ... she burns everything in her path, like the fire in a forge.

So while we lived without concern, considering your marriage a problem of the past, Mawdo's mother thought day and night of a way to get her revenge on you, the goldsmith's daughter.

One fine day she decided to pay a visit to her younger brother, Farba Diouf, a customary chief in Diakhao. She packed a few well chosen clothes into a suitcase that she borrowed from me, stuffed a basket full of various purchases: provisions and foodstuffs that are dear or rare in the Sine (fruits from France, cheese, preserves), toys for nephews, lengths of material for her brother and his four wives.

She asked Modou for some money, which she carefully folded and put away in her purse. She had her hair done, painted her feet and hands with henna. Thus dressed, adorned, she left.

These days, the road to Rufisque forks at the Diamniadio crossroads: the National 1, to the right, leads, after Mbour, to the Sine-Saloum, while the National 2 goes through Thies and Tivaouane, cradle of Tidjanism, towards Saint-Louis, former capital of Senegal. Aunty Nabou did not enjoy the benefit of these pleasant roads. Jostled in the bus on the bumpy road, she sought refuge in her memories. The dizzying speed of the vehicle, carrying her towards the place of her childhood, did not prevent her from recognizing the familiar countryside. Here, Sindia, and to the left, Popenguine, where the Catholics celebrate Whitsun.

How many generations has this same unchanging countryside seen glide past! Aunty Nabou acknowledged man's vulnerability in the face of the eternity of nature. By its very duration, nature defies time and takes its revenge on man.

The baobab trees held out the giant knots of their branches towards the skies; slowly, the cows moved across the road, their mournful stare defying the vehicles; shepherds in baggy trousers, their sticks on their shoulders or in their hands, guided the animals. Men and animals blended, as in a picture risen from the depths of time.

Aunty Nabou closed her eyes every time the bus passed another vehicle. She was especially frightened of the big lorries with their huge loads.

The beautiful Medinatou-Minaouara mosque had not yet been built to the glory of Islam, but in the same pious spirit, men and women prayed by the side of the road. 'You have to come away from Dakar to be convinced of the survival of traditions,' murmured Aunty Nabou.

On the left, prickly shrubs bordered the Ndiassane forest; monkeys darted out to enjoy the light.

Thiadiaye, Tataguine, Diouroupe, then Ndioudiouf, and finally Fatick, capital of the Sine. Puffing and steaming, the bus branched off to the left. Jolts and still more jolts. Finally Diakhao, the royal Diakhao, Diakhao, cradle and tomb of the Bour-Sine, Diakhao of her ancestors, beloved Diakhao, with the vast compound of its old palace.

The same heaviness tortured her heart on each visit paid to the family domain.

First of all, water for ablutions and a mat on which to pray and to meditate before the tomb of the ancestor. And then she let her gaze, marked with sadness and filled with history, roam over the other tombs. Here, the dead and the living lived together in the family compound: each king, returned from his coronation, planted two trees in the yard that marked out his last resting place. Fervently, Aunty Nabou intoned the religious verses, directing them at the tombs of the dead. Her face wore a tragic mask in this place of grandeur, which sang of the past to the sound of the *djou-*

djoungs, the royal drums.

She swore that your existence, Aissatou, would never tarnish her noble descent.

Associating in her thoughts antiquated rites and religion, she remembered the milk to be poured into the Sine[11] to appease the invisible spirits. Tomorrow, in the river, she would make her offerings to protect herself from the evil eye, while at the same time attracting the benevolence of the *tours*[12].

Royally received, she immediately resumed her position as the elder sister of the master of the house. Nobody addressed her without kneeling down. She took her meals alone, having been served with the choicest bits from the pots.

Visitors came from everywhere to honour her, thus reminding her of the truth of the law of blood. For her, they revived the exploits of the ancestor Bour-Sine, the dust of combats and the ardour of thoroughbred horses ... And, heady with the heavy scent of burnt incense, she drew force and vigour from the ancestral ashes stirred to the eclectic sound of the *koras*. She summoned her brother.

'I need a child beside me,' she said, 'to fill my heart. I want this child to be both my legs and my right arm. I am growing old. I will make of this child another me. Since the marriage of my own children, the house has been empty.'

She was thinking of you, working out her vengeance, but was very careful not to speak of you, of her hatred for you.

'Let your wish be fulfilled,' replied Farba Diouf. 'I have never asked you to educate any of my daughters, not wanting to tire you. Yet today's children are difficult to keep in check. Take young Nabou, your namesake. She is yours. I ask only for her bones.'

Satisfied, Aunty Nabou packed her suitcase again, filled her basket with all that could be found in the village and is dear in town: dried couscous, roasted groundnut paste, millet, eggs, milk, chicken. Holding young Nabou's hand firmly in her right hand, she took the road back to town.

12

As she handed me back my suitcase, Aunty Nabou introduced young Nabou to me; she also introduced her at the homes of all her friends.

With my help, young Nabou was admitted into the French school. Maturing in her aunt's protective shade, she learned the secret of making delicious sauces, of using an iron and wielding a pestle. Her aunt never missed an opportunity to remind her of her royal origin, and taught her that the first quality in a woman is docility.

After obtaining her primary school certificate, and after a few years in secondary school, the older Nabou advised her niece to sit the entrance examination for the State School of Midwifery: 'This school is good. You receive an education there. No garlands for heads. Young, sober girls without earrings, dressed in white, which is the colour of purity. The profession you will learn there is a beautiful one; you will earn your living and you will acquire grace for your entry into paradise by helping at the birth of new followers of Mohammed, the Prophet. To tell the truth, a woman does not need too much education. In fact, I wonder how a woman can earn her living by talking from morning to night.'

Thus, young Nabou became a midwife. One fine day, Aunty Nabou called Mawdo and said to him: 'My brother Farba has given you young Nabou to be your wife, to thank me for the worthy way in which I have brought her up. I will never get over it if you don't take her as your wife. Shame kills faster than disease.'

I knew about it. Modou knew about it. The whole town knew about it. You, Aissatou, suspected nothing and continued to be radiant.

And because his mother had fixed a date for the wedding night, Mawdo finally had the courage to tell you what every woman was whispering: you had a co-wife. 'My mother is old. The knocks and disappointments of life have weakened her heart. If I spurn this child, she will die. This is the doctor speaking and not the son. Think of it, her brother's daughter, brought up by her, rejected by her son. What shame before society!'

It was 'so as not to see his mother die of shame and chagrin' that Mawdo agreed to go to the rendezvous of the wedding night. Faced with this rigid mother moulded by the old morality, burning with the fierce ardour of antiquated laws, what could Mawdo Bâ do? He was getting on in years, worn out by his arduous work. And then, did he really want to fight, to make a gesture of resistance? Young Nabou was so tempting ...

From then on, you no longer counted. What of the time and the love you had invested in your home? Only trifles, quickly forgotten. Your sons? They counted for very little in this reconciliation between a mother and her 'one and only man'; you no longer counted, any more than did your four sons: they could never be equal to young Nabou's sons.

The *griots* spoke of young Nabou's sons, exalting them: 'Blood has returned to its source.'

Your sons did not count. Mawdo's mother, a princess, could not recognize herself in the sons of a goldsmith's daughter.

In any case, could a goldsmith's daughter have any dignity, any honour? This was tantamount to asking whether you had a heart and flesh. Ah! for some people the honour and chagrin of a goldsmith's daughter count for less, much less, than the honour and chagrin of a *Guelewar*.

Mawdo did not drive you away. He did his duty and wished that you would stay on. Young Nabou would continue to live with his mother; it was you he loved. Every other night he would go to his mother's place to see his other wife, so that his mother 'would not die', to 'fulfil a duty'.

31

How much greater you proved to be than those who sapped your happiness!

You were advised to compromise: 'You don't burn the tree which bears the fruit.'

You were threatened through your flesh: 'Boys cannot succeed without their father.'

You took no notice.

These commonplace truths, which before had lowered the heads of many wives as they raised them in revolt, did not produce the desired miracle; they did not divert you from your decision. You chose to make a break, a one-way journey with your four sons, leaving this letter for Mawdo, in clear view, on the bed that used to be yours. I remember the exact words:

Mawdo,

Princes master their feelings to fulfil their duties. 'Others' bend their heads and, in silence, accept a destiny that oppresses them.

That, briefly put, is the internal ordering of our society, with its absurd divisions. I will not yield to it. I cannot accept what you are offering me today in place of the happiness we once had. You want to draw a line between heartfelt love and physical love. I say that there can be no union of bodies without the heart's acceptance, however little that may be.

If you can procreate without loving, merely to satisfy the pride of your declining mother, then I find you despicable. At that moment you tumbled from the highest rung of respect on which I have always placed you. Your reasoning, which makes a distinction, is unacceptable to me: on one side, me, 'your life, your love, your choice', on the other, 'young Nabou, to be tolerated for reasons of duty'.

Mawdo, man is one: greatness and animal fused together. None of his acts is pure charity. None is pure bestiality.

I am stripping myself of your love, your name. Clothed in my dignity, the only worthy garment, I go my way.

Goodbye,
Aissatou

And you left. You had the surprising courage to take your life into your own hands. You rented a house and set up home there. And instead of looking backwards, you looked resolutely to the future. You set yourself a difficult task; and more than just my presence and my encouragements, books saved you. Having become your refuge, they sustained you.

The power of books, this marvellous invention of astute human intelligence. Various signs associated with sound: different sounds that form the word. Juxtaposition of words from which springs the idea, Thought, History, Science, Life. Sole instrument of interrelationships and of culture, unparalleled means of giving and receiving. Books knit generations together in the same continuing effort that leads to progress. They enabled you to better yourself. What society refused you, they granted: examinations sat and passed took you also to France. The School of Interpreters, from which you graduated, led to your appointment in the Senegalese Embassy in the United States. You make a very good living. You are developing in peace, as your letters tell me, your back resolutely turned on those seeking light enjoyment and easy relationships.

And Mawdo? He renewed his relationship with his family. Those from Diakhao invaded his house: those from Diakhao sustained young Nabou. But – and Mawdo knew it – there was no possible comparison between yourself and young Nabou; you, so beautiful and so gentle, you, whose tenderness for him was so deep and disinterested, you, who knew how to mop your husband's brow, you, who could always find the right words with which to make him relax.

And Mawdo? What didn't he say? ' I am completely disorientated. You can't change the habits of a grown man. I look for shirts and trousers in the old places and I touch only emptiness.'

I had no pity for Mawdo.

'My house is a suburb of Diakhao. I find it impossible to get any rest there. Everything there is dirty. Young Nabou gives my food and my clothes away to visitors.'

I did not listen to Mawdo.

'Somebody told me he'd seen you with Aissatou yesterday. Is it true? Is she around? How is she? What about my sons?' I did not answer Mawdo.

For Mawdo, and through him all men, remained an enigma to me. Your departure had truly shaken him. His sadness was clearly evident. When he spoke of you, the inflexions in his voice hardened. But his disillusioned air, the bitter criticisms of his home, his wit, which railed at everything, did not in the least prevent the periodic swelling of young Nabou's belly. Two boys had already been born.

When faced with this visible fact, proof of his intimate relations with young Nabou, Mawdo would twist with anger. His look was like a whip: 'Look here, don't be an idiot. How can you expect a man to remain a stone when he is constantly in contact with the woman who runs his house?' He added as illustration: 'I saw a film in which the survivors of an air crash survived by eating the flesh of the corpses. This fact demonstrates the force of the

34

instincts in man, instincts that dominate him, regardless of his level of intelligence. Slough off this surfeit of dreamy sentimentality. Accept reality in its crude ugliness.'

'You can't resist the imperious laws that demand food and clothing for man. These same laws compel the "male" in other respects. I say "male" to emphasize the bestiality of instincts ... You understand ... A wife must understand, once and for all, and must forgive; she must not worry herself about "betrayals of the flesh". The important thing is what there is in the heart; that's what unites two beings inside.' (He struck his chest, at the point where the heart lies.)

'Driven to the limits of my resistance, I satisfy myself with what is within reach. It's a terrible thing to say. Truth is ugly when one analyses it.'

Thus, to justify himself, he reduced young Nabou to a 'plate of food'. Thus, for the sake of 'variety', men are unfaithful to their wives.

I was irritated. He was asking me to understand. But to understand what? The supremacy of instinct? The right to betray? The justification of the desire for variety? I could not be an ally to polygamic instincts. What, then, was I to understand?

How I envied your calmness during your last visit! There you were, rid of the mask of suffering. Your sons were growing up well, contrary to all predictions. You did not care about Mawdo. Yes, indeed, there you were, the past crushed beneath your heel. There you were, an innocent victim of an unjust cause and the courageous pioneer of a new life.

13

My own crisis came three years after yours. But unlike your case, the source was not my family-in-law. The problem was rooted in Modou himself, my husband.

My daughter Daba, who was preparing for her *baccalauréat*, often brought some of her classmates home with her. Most of the time it was the same young girl, a bit shy, frail, made noticeably uncomfortable by our style of life. But she was really beautiful in this her adolescent period, in her faded but clean clothes! Her beauty shone, pure. Her shapely contours could not but be noticed.

I sometimes noticed that Modou was interested in the pair. Neither was I worried when I heard him suggest that he should take Binetou home in the car – 'because it was getting late,' he would say.

Binetou was going through a metamorphosis, however. She was now wearing very expensive off-the-peg dresses. Smilingly, she would explain to my daughter: 'Oh, I have a sugar-daddy who pays for them.'

Then one day, on her return from school, Daba confided to me that Binetou had a serious problem: 'The sugar-daddy of the boutique dresses wants to marry Binetou. Just imagine. Her parents want to withdraw her from school, with only a few months to go before the *bac*, to marry her off to the sugar-daddy.'

'Advise her to refuse,' I said.

'And if the man in question offers her a villa, Mecca for her parents, a car, a monthly allowance, jewels?'

'None of that is worth the capital of youth.'

'I agree with you, Mum. I'll tell Binetou not to give in; but her mother is a woman who wants so much to escape from mediocrity and who regrets so much her past beauty, faded in the smoke from the wood fires, that she looks enviously at everything I wear; she complains all day long.'

'What is important is Binetou herself. She must not give in.'

And then, a few days afterwards, Daba renewed the conversation, with its surprising conclusion.

'Mum! Binetou is heartbroken. She is going to marry her sugar-daddy. Her mother cried so much. She begged her daughter to give her life a happy end, in a proper house, as the man has promised them. So she accepted.'

'When is the wedding?'

'This coming Sunday, but there'll be no reception. Binetou cannot bear the mockery of her friends.'

And in the evening of this same Sunday on which Binetou was being married off I saw come into my house, all dressed up and solemn, Tamsir, Modou's brother, with Mawdo Bâ and his local *Imam*. Where had they come from, looking so awkward in their starched *boubous*? Doubtless, they had come looking for Modou to carry out an important task that one of them had been charged with. I told them that Modou had been out since morning. They entered laughing, deliberately sniffing the fragrant odour of incense that was floating on the air. I sat in front of them, laughing with them. The *Imam* attacked:

'There is nothing one can do when Allah the almighty puts two people side by side.'

'True, true,' said the other two in support.

A pause. He took a breath and continued: 'There is nothing new in this world.'

'True, true,' Tamsir and Mawdo chimed in again.

'Some things we may find to be sad are much less so than others ...'

I followed the movement of the haughty lips that let fall these axioms, which can precede the announcement of either a happy event or an unhappy one. What was he leading up to with these preliminaries that rather announced a storm? So their visit was obviously planned.

Does one announce bad news dressed up like that in one's Sunday best? Or did they want to inspire confidence with their impeccable dress?

I thought of the absent one. I asked with the cry of a hunted beast: 'Modou?'

And the *Imam*, who had finally got hold of a leading thread, held tightly on to it. He went on quickly, as if the words were glowing embers in his mouth: 'Yes, Modou Fall, but, happily, he is alive for you, for all of us, thanks be to God. All he has done is to marry a second wife today. We have just come from the mosque in Grand Dakar where the marriage took place.'

The thorns thus removed from the way, Tamsir ventured: 'Modou sends his thanks. He says it is fate that decides men and things: God intended him to have a second wife, there is nothing he can do about it. He praises you for the quarter of a century of marriage in which you gave him all the happiness a wife owes her husband. His family, especially myself, his elder brother, thank you. You have always held us in respect. You know that we are Modou's blood.'

Afterwards there were the same old words, which were intended to relieve the situation: 'You are the only one in your house, no matter how big it is, no matter how dear life is. You are the first wife, a mother for Modou, a friend for Modou.'

Tamsir's Adam's apple danced about in his throat. He shook his left leg, crossed over his folded right leg. His shoes, white Turkish slippers, were covered with a thin layer of red dust, the colour of the earth in which they had walked. The same dust covered Mawdo's and the *Imam*'s shoes.

Mawdo said nothing. He was reliving his own experience. He was thinking of your letter, your reaction, and you and I were so alike. He was being wary. He kept his head lowered, in the attitude of those who accept defeat before the battle.

I acquiesced under the drops of poison that were burning

me: 'A quarter of a century of marriage', 'a wife unparalleled'. I counted backwards to determine where the break in the thread had occurred from which everything had unwound. My mother's words came back to me: 'too perfect...' I completed at last my mother's thought with the end of the dictum: ' ... to be honest'. I thought of the first two incisors with a wide gap between them, the sign of the primacy of love in the individual. I thought of his absence, all day long. He had simply said: 'Don't expect me for lunch.' I thought of other absences, quite frequent these days, crudely clarified today yet well hidden yesterday under the guise of trade union meetings. He was also on a strict diet, 'to break the stomach's egg,' he would say laughingly, this egg that announced old age.

Every night when he went out he would unfold and try on several of his suits before settling on one. The others, impatiently rejected, would slip to the floor. I would have to fold them again and put them back in their places; and this extra work, I discovered, I was doing only to help him in his effort to be elegant in his seduction of another woman.

I forced myself to check my inner agitation. Above all, I must not give my visitors the pleasure of relating my distress. Smile, take the matter lightly, just as they announced it. Thank them for the humane way in which they have accomplished their mission. Send thanks to Modou, 'a good father and a good husband', 'a husband become a friend'. Thank my family-in-law, the *Imam*, Mawdo. Smile. Give them something to drink. See them out, under the swirls of incense that they were sniffing once again. Shake their hands.

How pleased they were, all except Mawdo, who correctly judged the import of the event.

14

Alone at last, able to give free rein to my surprise and to gauge my distress. Ah! yes, I forgot to ask for my rival's name so that I might give a human form to my pain.

My question was soon answered. Acquaintances from Grand Dakar came rushing to my house, bringing the various details of the ceremony. Some of them did so out of true friendship for me; others were spiteful and jealous of the promotion Binetou's mother would gain from the marriage.

'I don't understand.' They did not understand either the entrance of Modou, a 'personality', into this extremely poor family.

Binetou, a child the same age as my daughter Daba, promoted to the rank of my co-wife, whom I must face up to. Shy Binetou! The old man who bought her the new off-the-peg dresses to replace the old faded ones was none other than Modou. She had innocently confided her secrets to her rival's daughter because she thought that this dream, sprung from a brain growing old, would never become reality. She had told everything: the villa, the monthly allowance, the offer of a future trip to Mecca for her parents. She thought she was stronger than the man she was dealing with. She did not know Modou's strong will, his tenacity before an obstacle, the pride he invests in winning, the resistance that inspires new attempts at each failure.

Daba was furious, her pride wounded. She repeated all the nicknames Binetou had given her father: old man, pot-belly, sugar-daddy! ... the person who gave her life had been daily ridiculed and he accepted it. An overwhelming anger raged inside Daba. She knew that her best friend was sincere in what she said. But what can a child do, faced with a furious mother shouting about her hunger and her thirst to live?

Binetou, like many others, was a lamb slaughtered on the

altar of affluence. Daba's anger increased as she analysed the situation: 'Break with him, mother! Send this man away. He has respected neither you nor me. Do what Aunty Aissatou did; break with him. Tell me you'll break with him. I can't see you fighting over a man with a girl my age.'

I told myself what every betrayed woman says: if Modou was milk, it was I who had had all the cream. The rest, well, nothing but water with a vague smell of milk.

But the final decision lay with me. With Modou absent all night (was he already consummating his marriage?), the solitude that lends counsel enabled me to grasp the problem.

Leave? Start again at zero, after living twenty-five years with one man, after having borne twelve children? Did I have enough energy to bear alone the weight of this responsibility, which was both moral and material?

Leave! Draw a clean line through the past. Turn over a page on which not everything was bright, certainly, but at least all was clear. What would now be recorded there would hold no love, confidence, grandeur or hope. I had never known the sordid side of marriage. Don't get to know it! Run from it! When one begins to forgive, there is an avalanche of faults that comes crashing down, and the only thing that remains is to forgive again, to keep on forgiving. Leave, escape from betrayal! Sleep without asking myself any questions, without straining my ear at the slightest noise, waiting for a husband I share.

I counted the abandoned or divorced women of my generation whom I knew.

I knew a few whose remaining beauty had been able to capture a worthy man, a man who added fine bearing to a good situation and who was considered 'better, a hundred times better than his predecessor'. The misery that was the lot of these women was rolled back with the invasion of the new happiness that changed their lives, filled out their cheeks, brightened their eyes. I knew others who had lost all hope of renewal and whom loneliness had very quickly laid underground.

The play of destiny remains impenetrable. The cowries that a female neighbour throws on a fan in front of me do not fill me with optimism, neither when they remain face upwards, showing the black hollow that signifies laughter, nor when the grouping of their white backs seems to say that 'the man in the double trousers'[13] is coming towards me, the promise of wealth. 'The only thing that separates you from them, man and wealth, is the alms of two white and red cola nuts,' adds Farmata, my neighbour.

She insists: 'There is a saying that discord here may be luck elsewhere. Why are you afraid to make the break? A woman is like a ball; once a ball is thrown, no one can predict where it will bounce. You have no control over where it rolls, and even less over who gets it. Often it is grabbed by an unexpected hand ...'

Instead of listening to the reasoning of my neighbour, a *griot* woman who dreams of the generous tips due to the go-between, I looked at myself in the mirror. My eyes took in the mirror's eloquence. I had lost my slim figure, as well as ease and quickness of movement. My stomach protruded from beneath the wrapper that hid the calves developed by the impressive number of kilometres walked since the beginning of my existence. Suckling had robbed my breasts of their round firmness. I could not delude myself: youth was deserting my body.

Whereas a woman draws from the passing years the force of her devotion, despite the ageing of her companion, a man, on the other hand, restricts his field of tenderness. His egoistic eye looks over his partner's shoulder. He compares what he had with what he no longer has, what he has with what he could have.

I had heard of too many misfortunes not to understand my own. There was your own case, Aissatou, the cases of many other women, despised, relegated or exchanged, who were abandoned like a worn-out or out-dated *boubou*.

To overcome distress when it sits upon you demands strong will. When one thinks that with each passing second one's life is shortened, one must profit intensely from this second; it is the sum of all the lost or harvested seconds that makes for a wasted or a successful life. Brace oneself to check despair and get it into proportion! A nervous breakdown waits around the corner for anyone who lets himself wallow in bitterness. Little by little, it takes over your whole being.

Oh, nervous breakdown! Doctors speak of it in a detached, ironical way, emphasizing that the vital organs are in no way disturbed. You are lucky if they don't tell you that you are wasting their time with the ever-growing list of your illnesses – your head, throat, chest, heart, liver – that no X-ray can confirm. And yet what atrocious suffering is caused by nervous breakdowns!

And I think of Jacqueline, who suffered from one. Jacqueline, the Ivorian, had disobeyed her Protestant parents and had married Samba Diack, a contemporary of Mawdo Bâ's, a doctor like him, who, on leaving the African School of Medicine and Pharmacy, was posted to Abidjan. Jacqueline often came round to see us, since her husband often visited our household. Coming to Senegal, she found herself in a new world, a world with different reactions, temperament and mentality from that in which she had grown up. In addition, her husband's relatives – always the relatives – were cool towards her because she refused to adopt the Muslim religion and went instead to the Protestant church every Sunday.

A black African, she should have been able to fit without difficulty into a black African society, Senegal and the Ivory Coast both having experienced the same colonial power. But Africa is diverse, divided. The same country can change its character and outlook several times over, from north to south or from east to west.

Jacqueline truly wanted to become Senegalese, but the mockery checked all desire in her to co-operate. People called her

43

gnac[14], and she finally understood the meaning of this nickname that revolted her so.

Her husband, making up for lost time, spent his time chasing slender Senegalese women, as he would say with appreciation, and did not bother to hide his adventures, respecting neither his wife nor his children. His lack of precautions brought to Jacqueline's knowledge the irrefutable proof of his misconduct: love notes, cheque stubs bearing the names of the payees, bills from restaurants and for hotel rooms. Jacqueline cried; Samba Diack 'lived it up'. Jacqueline lost weight; Samba Diack was still living fast. Jacqueline complained of a disturbing lump in her chest, under her left breast; she said she had the impression that a sharp point had pierced her there and was cutting through her flesh right to her very bones. She fretted. Mawdo listened to her heart: nothing wrong there, he would say. He prescribed some tranquillizers. Eagerly, Jacqueline took the tablets, tortured by the insidious pain. The bottle empty, she noticed that the lump remained in the same place; she continued to feel the pain just as acutely as ever.

She consulted a doctor from her own country, who ordered an electrocardiogram and various blood tests. Nothing to be learned from the electric reading of the heart, nothing abnormal found in the blood. He too prescribed tranquillizers, big, effervescent tablets that could not allay poor Jacqueline's distress.

She thought of her parents, of their refusal to consent to her marriage. She wrote them a pathetic letter, in which she begged for their forgiveness. They sent their sincere blessing but could do nothing to lighten the strange weight in her chest.

◊

Jacqueline was taken to Fann Hospital on the road to Ouakam, near the university, where medical students do their internship, as they do at the Aristide Le Dantec Hospital. This hospital did not

44

exist at the time Mawdo Bâ and Samba Diack studied at the School of Medicine and Pharmacy. It has many departments, housed either in separate buildings or in adjoining ones to facilitate communication. These buildings, despite their number and size, do not manage to fill up the hospital's vast grounds. On entering it, Jacqueline thought of those gone mad, confined inside. It was necessary to explain to her that the mad ones were in psychiatric care and that here they were called the mentally sick and, in any case, were not violent, the violent ones being confined in the psychiatric hospital at Thiaroye. Jacqueline was in a neurology ward, and those of us who went to visit her learned that the hospital also had departments for treating tuberculosis and infectious diseases.

Jacqueline lay prostrate in her bed. Her beautiful but neglected black hair, through which no comb had been run ever since she began consulting doctor after doctor, formed shaggy tufts on her head. When the scarf protecting it slipped out of place, it would uncover the coating of a mixture of roots that we poured on her, for we tried everything to draw this sister out of her private hell. And it was your mother, Aissatou, who went to consult the native medicine men for us and brought back *safara*[15] from her visits and directions for the sacrifices you quickly carried out.

Jacqueline's thoughts turned to death. She waited for it, frightened and tormented, her hand on her chest, where the tenacious, invisible lump foiled all the ruses, scoffed maliciously at all the tranquillizers. Jacqueline's room-mate was a French Technical Co-operation teacher of literature, posted to the Lycée Faidherbe in Saint-Louis. The only thing she knew of Saint-Louis, she said, was the bridge that spanned the river. A sore throat, an affliction as sudden as it was violent, had prevented her from taking up her duties and had brought her here, where she was waiting to be repatriated.

I observed her often. Old, for her unmarried status. Thin,

45

angular even, without any charm. Her studies must have been her only form of recreation during her youth. Sour-tempered, she must have put off any passionate advances. It was perhaps her loneliness that had made her seek for a change. A teaching post in Senegal must have corresponded to her dreams of escape. She had come therefore, but all her frustrated dreams, all her disappointed hopes, all her crushed revolt connived to attack her throat, protected by a navy-blue scarf with white dots, which contrasted with the pale-ness of her chest. The medication with which her throat was paint-ed gave a blueish tint to her thin lips, pinched over their misery. She had big, luminous, blue eyes, the only light, the only point of beauty, the only heavenly grace in her ungracious face. She tapped against her throat; Jacqueline tapped against her chest. We would laugh at their ways, especially when the patient from the next room came to 'chat', as she said, and would uncover her back for the refreshing caress of the air-conditioner. She suffered from sudden flushes, which burned her terribly at this spot.

Strange and varied manifestations of neuro-vegetative dystonia. Doctors, beware, especially if you are neurologists or psychiatrists. Often, the pains you are told of have their roots in moral torment. Vexations suffered and constant frustrations: these are what accumulate somewhere in the body and choke it.

Jacqueline, who enjoyed life, bravely endured blood test after blood test. Another electrocardiogram, another X-ray of the lungs. An electro-encephalogram was carried out, which revealed traces of her suffering. It then became necessary to do a gaseous electro-encephalography. This is extremely painful, always entailing a lumbar puncture. That day, Jacqueline remained confined to bed, looking more pitiful and haggard than ever before.

Samba Diack was kind and touched by his wife's breakdown.

One fine day, after a month of treatment (intravenous injections and tranquillizers), after a month of investigations, during which her French neighbour had returned to her country,

46

the doctor who was head of the Neurology Department asked to see Jacqueline. She found in front of her a man whom maturity and the nobility of his job had made even more attractive, a man who had not been hardened by constant dealing with the most deplorable of miseries, that of mental alienation. With his sharp eyes, accustomed to judging, he looked into those of Jacqueline in order to discover in her soul the source of the distress disrupting her organism. In a soft, reassuring voice, which in itself was balm to this overstrung being, he explained: 'Madame Diack, I assure you that there is nothing at all wrong with your head. The X-rays have shown nothing, and neither have the blood tests. The problem is that you are depressed, that is ... not happy. You wish the conditions of life were different from what they are in reality, and this is what is torturing you. Moreover, you had your babies too soon after each other; the body loses its vital juices, which haven't had the time to be replaced. In short, there is nothing endangering your life.

'You must react, go out, give yourself a reason for living. Take courage. Slowly, you will overcome. We will give you a series of shock treatments with curare to relax you. You can leave afterwards.'

The doctor punctuated his words by nodding his head and smiling convincingly, giving Jacqueline much hope. Reanimated, she related the discussion to us and confided that she had left the interview already half-cured. She knew the heart of her illness and would fight against it. She was morally uplifted. She had come a long way, had Jacqueline!

Why did I recall this friend's ordeal? Was it because of its happy ending? Or merely to delay the formulation of the choice I had made, a choice that my reason rejected but that accorded with the immense tenderness I felt towards Modou Fall?

Yes, I was well aware of where the right solution lay, the dignified solution. And, to my family's great surprise, unanimously

47

disapproved of by my children, who were under Daba's influence, I chose to remain. Modou and Mawdo were surprised, could not understand ...

Forewarned, you, my friend, did not try to dissuade me, respectful of my new choice of life.

I cried every day.

From then on, my life changed. I had prepared myself for equal sharing, according to the precepts of Islam concerning polygamic life. I was left with empty hands.

My children, who disagreed with my decision, sulked. In opposition to me, they represented a majority I had to respect.

'You have not finished suffering,' predicted Daba.

I lived in a vacuum. And Modou avoided me. Attempts by friends and family to bring him back to the fold proved futile. One of the new couple's neighbours explained to me that the 'child' would go 'all a-quiver' each time Modou said my name or showed any desire to see his children. He never came again; his new-found happiness gradually swallowed up his memory of us. He forgot about us.

15

Aissatou, my dear friend, I've told you that there can be no possible comparison between you and young Nabou. But I also realize that there can be no possible comparison between young Nabou and Binetou. Young Nabou grew up beside her aunt, who had earmarked her as the spouse of her son Mawdo. Used to seeing him, she let herself be drawn towards him, naturally, without any shock. His greying hair did not offend her; she found his thickening features reassuring. And then she loved and still loves Mawdo, even if their interests are not always the same.

School had not left a strong mark on young Nabou, preceded and dominated as it was by the strength of character of Aunty Nabou, who, in her rage for vengeance, had left nothing to chance in the education she gave her niece. It was especially while telling folk tales, late at night under the starlit sky, that Aunty Nabou wielded her power over young Nabou's soul: her expressive voice glorified the retributive violence of the warrior; her expressive voice lamented the anxiety of the Loved One, all submissive. She saluted the courage of the reckless; she stigmatized trickery, laziness, calumny; she demanded care of the orphan and respect for old age. Tales with animal characters, nostalgic songs kept young Nabou breathless. And slowly but surely, through the sheer force of repetition, the virtues and greatness of a race took root in this child.

This kind of oral education, easily assimilated, full of charm, has the power to bring out the best in the adult mind, developed in its contact with it. Softness and generosity, docility and politeness, poise and tact, all these qualities made young Nabou pleasant. Mawdo used to call her 'finicky', with a shrug of his shoulders.

And then, young Nabou had a profession. She had no time to worry about her 'state of mind'. In charge of frequent shifts at the 'Repos Mandel' Maternity Home, on the outskirts of the crowded and badly serviced suburban areas, all day and several times over she would go through the same gestures engendering life. Babies passed again and again between her expert hands.

She would come back from work railing at the lack of beds that led to the discharge, too early in her opinion, of the new mothers; worried about the lack of staff, inadequate instruments, medicines. She would say, with deep concern: 'The fragile baby is let loose too quickly into a hygienically unsound social environment.'

She thought of the great rate of infant mortality, which nights of care and devotion cannot decrease. She thought: What a thrilling adventure it is to turn a baby into a healthy man. But how many mothers are able to accomplish that feat?

In the midst of life, in the midst of poverty, in the midst of ugliness, young Nabou would often triumph with her knowledge and experience; but she sometimes knew heartrending failure; she remained powerless, faced with the force of death.

Young Nabou, responsible and aware, like you, like me! Even though she is not my friend, we often shared the same problems.

She found life hard and, being a fighter, had not the least inclination for frivolities.

As for Binetou, she had grown up in complete liberty in an environment where survival was of the essence. Her mother was more concerned with putting the pot on the boil than with education. Beautiful, lively, kindhearted, intelligent, Binetou had access to many of her friends' well-off families and was sharply aware of what she was sacrificing by her marriage. A victim, she wanted to be the oppressor. Exiled in the world of adults, which was not her own, she wanted her prison gilded. Demanding, she tormented. Sold, she raised her price daily. What she renounced, those things which before used to be the sap of her life and which she would bitterly enumerate, called for exorbitant compensations, which Modou exhausted himself trying to provide. Echoes of her life would reach me, amplified or muted according to the visitor. The seductive power of mature age, of silvery temples, was un-known to Binetou. And Modou would dye his hair every month. His waistline painfully restrained by old-fashioned trousers, Binetou would never miss a chance of laughing wickedly at him. Modou would leave himself winded trying to imprison youth in its decline, which abandoned him on all sides: the graceless sag of a double chin, the gait hesitant and heavy at the slightest cool breeze. Gracefulness and beauty surrounded him. He was afraid of disappointing, and so that there would be no time for close scrutiny of him, he would create daily celebrations during which the bright young thing would move, an elf with slender arms who with a laugh could make life beautiful or with a pout bring sadness.

People talked of bewitchment. With determination, friends begged me to react: 'You are letting someone else pluck the fruits of your labour.'

Vehemently, they recommended *marabouts*, sure in their science, who had proved themselves by bringing husbands back to the fold, by separating them from evil women. These charlatans lived far away. Casamance was mentioned, where the Diola and Madjago excel in magic philtres. They suggested Linguere, the country of the Fulba, quick in vengeance through charms as through arms. They also talked of Mali, the country of the Bambara, with faces deeply scarred with tribal marks.

To act as I was urged would have been to call myself into question. I was already reproaching myself for a weakness that had not prevented the degradation of my home. Was I to deny myself because Modou had chosen another path? No, I would not give in to the pressure. My mind and my faith rejected supernatural power. They rejected this easy attraction, which kills any will to fight. I looked reality in the face.

Reality had the face of Lady Mother-in-Law, swallowing up double mouthfuls from the trough offered her. Her hunch about a gilded way of life was being proved right. Her unsteady hut, with zinc walls covered with magazine pages where pin-ups and advertisements were placed side by side, had grown dim in her memory. One motion of her hand in her bathroom and delicious jets of hot water would massage her back. Another in the kitchen and ice cubes would cool the water in her glass. One more and a flame would spring from the gas cooker and she would prepare herself a delicious omelette.

51

The senior wife hitherto neglected, Lady Mother-in-Law emerged from the shadows and took her unfaithful husband back in tow. She held valuable trump cards: grilled meats, roasted chicken and (why not?) banknotes slipped into the pockets of the *boubou* hanging in the bedroom. She no longer counted the cost of water bought from the Tukulor hawker of the vital liquid drawn from public springs. Having known poverty, she rejoiced in her new-found happiness. Modou fulfilled her expectations. He would thoughtfully send her wads of notes to spend and would offer her, after his trips abroad, jewellery and rich *boubous*. From then on, she joined the category of women 'with heavy bracelets' lauded by the *griots*. Thrilled, she would listen to the radio transmitting songs dedicated to her.

Her family reserved the best place for her during ceremonies and listened to her advice. When Modou's large car dropped her and she emerged, there would be a rush of outstretched hands into which she placed banknotes.

Reality was also Binetou, who went from night club to night club. She would arrive draped in a long, costly garment, a gold belt, a present from Modou on the birth of their first child, shining round her waist. Her shoes tapped on the ground, announcing her presence. The waiters would move aside and bow respectfully in the hope of a royal tip. With a contemptuous look, she would eye those already seated. With a pout like that of a spoilt child, she would indicate to Modou the table she had chosen. With a wave of her hand, like a magician, she would have various bottles lined up. She was showing off to the young people and wanted to impress them with her form of success. Binetou, incontestably beautiful and desirable! 'Bewitching,' people admitted. But when the moment of admiration passed, she was the one who lowered her head at the sight of couples graced with nothing but their youth and rich in their happiness alone.

The couples held each other or danced apart depending on

the music, sometimes slow and coaxing, sometimes vigorous and wild. When the trumpet blared out, backed by the frenzy of the drums, the young dancers, excited and untiring, would stamp, jump and caper about, shouting their joy. Modou would try to follow suit. The harsh lights betrayed him to the unpitying sarcasm of some of them, who called him a 'cradle-snatcher'. What did it matter! He had Binetou in his arms. He was happy.

Worn out, Binetou would watch with a disillusioned eye the progress of her friends. The image of her life, which she had murdered, broke her heart.

Sometimes also, despite my disapproval, Daba would go to the night clubs. Dressed simply, she would appear on her fiancé's arm; she would arrive late on purpose so as to sit in full view of her father. It was a grotesque confrontation: on one side, an ill-assorted couple, on the other two well-matched people.

And the evening created an extreme tension that opposed two former friends, a father and his daughter, a son-in-law and his father-in-law.

16

I was surviving. In addition to my former duties, I took over Modou's as well.

The purchase of basic foodstuffs kept me occupied at the end of every month; I made sure that I was never short of tomatoes or of oil, potatoes or onions during those periods when they became rare in the markets; I stored bags of 'Siam' rice, much loved by the Senegalese. My brain was taxed by new financial gymnastics.

The last date for payment of electricity bills and of water rates demanded my attention. I was often the only woman in the queue.

Replacing the locks and latches of broken doors, replacing broken windows was a bother, as well as looking for a plumber to deal with blocked sinks. My son Mawdo Fall complained about burnt-out bulbs that needed replacement.

I survived. I overcame my shyness at going alone to cinemas; I would take a seat with less and less embarrassment as the months went by. People stared at the middle-aged lady without a partner. I would feign indifference, while anger hammered against my nerves and the tears I held back welled up behind my eyes.

From the surprised looks, I gauged the slender liberty granted to women.

The early shows at the cinema filled me with delight. They gave me the courage to meet the curious gaze of various people. They did not keep me away for long from my children.

What a great distraction from distress is the cinema! Intellectual films, those with a message, sentimental films, detective films, comedies, thrillers, all these were my companions. I learned from them lessons of greatness, courage and perseverance. They deepened and widened my vision of the world, thanks to their cultural value. The cinema, an inexpensive means of recreation, can thus give healthy pleasure.

I survived. The more I thought about it, the more grateful I became to Modou for having cut off all contact. I had the solution my children wanted – the break without having taken the initiative. The lie had not taken root. Modou was excising me from his life and was proving it by his unequivocal attitude.

What do other husbands do? They wallow in indecision; they force themselves to be present where neither their feelings nor their interests continue to reside. Nothing impresses them in their home: the wife all dressed up, the son full of tenderness, the meal tastefully served. They remain stolid, like marble. They wish only that the hours may pass rapidly. At night, feigning fatigue or illness, they snore deeply. How quick they are to greet the liberating daybreak, which puts an end to their torment!

I was not deceived, therefore. I no longer interested Modou, and I knew it. I was abandoned: a fluttering leaf that no hand dares to pick up, as my grandmother would have said.

I faced up to the situation bravely. I carried out my duties; they filled the time and channelled my thoughts. But my loneliness would emerge at night, burdensome. One does not easily undo the tenuous ties that bind two people together during a journey fraught with hardship. I lived the proof of it, bringing back to life past scenes, past conversations. Our common habits sprang up at their usual times. I missed dreadfully our nightly conversation; I missed our bursts of refreshing or understanding laughter. Like opium, I missed our daily consultations. I pitted myself against shadows. The wanderings of my thoughts chased away all sleep. I side-stepped my pain in a refusal to fight it.

The continuity of radio broadcasts was a great relief. I gave the radio the role of comforter. At night the music lulled my anxiety. I heard the message of old and new songs, which awakened hope. My sadness dissolved.

With all the force I had, I called eagerly to 'another man' to replace Modou.

Distressing awakenings succeeded the nights. My love for my children sustained me. They were a pillar; I owed them help and affection.

Did Modou appreciate, in its full measure, the void created by his absence in this house? Did Modou attribute to me more energy than I had to shoulder the responsibility of my children?

I adopted a sprightly tone to rouse my battalion. The coffee warmed the atmosphere, exuding its sweet fragrance. Foaming baths, mutual teasing and laughter. A new day and increased efforts! A new day, and waiting ...

Waiting for what? It would not be easy to get my children to accept a new masculine presence. Having condemned their father, could they be tolerant towards another man? Besides, what man would have the courage to face twelve pairs of hostile eyes, which openly tear you apart?

Waiting! But waiting for what? I was not divorced ... I was abandoned: a fluttering leaf that no hand dares to pick up, as my grandmother would have said.

I survived. I experienced the inadequacy of public transport. My children laughed at themselves in making this harsh discovery. One day, I heard Daba advise them: 'Above all, don't let mum know that it is stifling in those buses during the rush hours.'

I shed tears of joy and sadness together: joy in being loved by my children, the sadness of a mother who does not have the means to change the course of events.

I told you then, without any ulterior motive, of this painful aspect of our life, while Modou's car drove Lady Mother-in-Law to the four corners of town and while Binetou streaked along the roads in an Alfa Romeo, sometimes white, sometimes red.

I shall never forget your response, you, my sister, nor my joy and my surprise when I was called to the Fiat agency and was told to choose a car which you had paid for, in full. My children gave cries of joy when they learned of the approaching end of their tribulations, which remain the daily lot of a good many other students.

Friendship has splendours that love knows not. It grows stronger when crossed, whereas obstacles kill love. Friendship resists time, which wearies and severs couples. It has heights unknown to love.

You, the goldsmith's daughter, gave me your help while depriving yourself.

And I learned to drive, stifling my fear. The narrow space between the wheel and the seat was mine. The flattened clutch glided in the gears. The brake reduced the forward thrust and, to speed along, I had to step on the accelerator. I did not trust the accelerator. At the slightest pressure from my feet, the car lurched forward. My feet learned to dance over the pedals. Whenever I was discouraged, I would say: Why should Binetou sit behind a wheel and not I? I would tell myself: Don't disappoint Aissatou. I won this battle of nerves and *sang-froid*. I obtained my driving licence and told you about it.

I told you: and now – my children on the backseat of the cream-coloured Fiat 125; thanks to you, my children can look the affluent mother-in-law and the fragile child in the eye in the streets of the town.

Modou surprised, unbelieving, inquired into the source of the car. He never accepted the true story. Like Mawdo's mother, he too believed that a goldsmith's daughter had no heart.

17

I take a deep breath.

I've related at one go your story as well as mine. I've said the essential, for pain, even when it's past, leaves the same marks on the individual when recalled. Your disappointment was mine, as my rejection was yours. Forgive me once again if I have re-opened your wound. Mine continues to bleed.

You may tell me: the path of life is not smooth; one is bruised by its sharp edges. I also know that marriage is never smooth. It reflects differences in character and capacity for feeling. In one couple the man may be the victim of a fickle woman or of a woman shut up in her own preoccupations who rejects all dialogue and quashes all moves towards tenderness. In another couple alcoholism is the leprosy that gnaws away at health, wealth and peace. It shows up an individual's disordered state through grotesque spectacles by which his dignity is undermined, in situations where physical blows become solid arguments and the menacing blade of a knife an irresistible call for silence.

With others it is the lure of easy gain that dominates: incorrigible players at the gaming table or seated in the shade of a tree. The heated atmosphere of rooms full of fiendish odours, the distorted faces of tense players. The giddy whirl of playing cards swallows up time, wealth, conscience, and stops only with the last breath of the person accustomed to shuffling them.

I try to spot my faults in the failure of my marriage. I gave freely, gave more than I received. I am one of those who can realize themselves fully and bloom only when they form part of a couple. Even though I understand your stand, even though I respect the choice of liberated women, I have never conceived of happiness outside marriage.

I loved my house. You can testify to the fact that I made it a haven of peace where everything had its place, that I created a harmonious symphony of colours. You know how soft-hearted I am, how much I loved Modou. You can testify to the fact that, mobilized day and night in his service, I anticipated his slightest desire.

I made peace with his family. Despite his desertion of our home, his father and mother and Tamsir, his brother, still continued to visit me often, as did his sisters. My children too grew up without much ado. Their success at school was my pride, just like laurels thrown at the feet of my lord and master.

And Modou was no prisoner. He spent his time as he wished. I well understood his desire to let off steam. He fulfilled himself outside as he wished in his trade union activities.

I am trying to pinpoint any weakness in the way I conducted myself. My social life may have been stormy and perhaps injured Modou's trade union career. Can a man, deceived and flouted by his family, impose himself on others? Can a man whose wife does not do her job well honestly demand a fair reward for labour?

Aggression and condescension in a woman arouse contempt and hatred for her husband. If she is gracious, even without appealing to any ideology, she can summon support for any action. In a word, a man's success depends on feminine support.

And I ask myself. I ask myself, why? Why did Modou detach himself? Why did he put Binetou between us?

You, very logically, may reply: 'Affections spring from nothing; sometimes a grimace, the carriage of a head can seduce a heart and keep it.'

I ask myself questions. The truth is that, despite everything, I remain faithful to the love of my youth. Aissatou, I cry for Modou, and I can do nothing about it.

18

Yesterday I celebrated, as is the custom, the fortieth day of Modou's death. I have forgiven him. May God hear the prayer I say for him every day. I celebrated the fortieth day in meditation. The initiated read the Koran. Their fervent voices rose towards heaven. Modou Fall, may God accept you among his chosen few.

After going through the motions of piety, Tamsir came and sat in my bedroom in the blue armchair that used to be your favourite. Sticking his head outside, he signalled to Mawdo; he also signalled to the *Imam* from the mosque in his area. The *Imam* and Mawdo joined him. This time, Tamsir speaks: There is a striking resemblance between Modou and Tamsir, the same tics donated by the inexplicable law of heredity. Tamsir speaks with great assurance; he touches, once again, on my years of marriage, then he concludes: 'When you have "come out" (that is to say, of mourning), I shall marry you. You suit me as a wife, and further, you will continue to live here, just as if Modou were not dead. Usually it is the younger brother who inherits his elder brother's wife. In this case, it is the opposite. You are my good luck. I shall marry you. I prefer you to the other one, too frivolous, too young. I advised Modou against that marriage.'

What a declaration of love, full of conceit, in a house still in mourning. What assurance and calm aplomb! I look Tamsir straight in the eye. I look at Mawdo. I look at the *Imam*. I draw my black shawl closer. I tell my beads. This time I shall speak out.

My voice has known thirty years of silence, thirty years of harassment. It bursts out, violent, sometimes sarcastic, sometimes contemptuous.

'Did you ever have any affection for your brother? Already you want to build a new home for yourself, over a body that is still warm. While we are praying for Modou, you are thinking of future wedding festivities.

'Ah, yes! Your strategy is to get in before any other suitor, to get in before Mawdo, the faithful friend, who has more qualities than you and who also, according to custom, can inherit the wife. You forget that I have a heart, a mind, that I am not an object to be passed from hand to hand. You don't know what marriage means to me: it is an act of faith and of love, the total surrender of oneself to the person one has chosen and who has chosen you.' (I emphasized the word 'chosen'.)

'What of your wives, Tamsir? Your income can meet neither their needs nor those of your numerous children. To help you out with your financial obligations, one of your wives dyes, another sells fruit, the third untiringly turns the handle of her sewing machine. You, the revered lord, you take it easy, obeyed at the crook of a finger. I shall never be the one to complete your collection. My house shall never be for you the coveted oasis: no extra burden; my "turn" every day;[16] cleanliness and luxury, abundance and calm! No, Tamsir!

'And then there are Daba and her husband, who have demon-

60

strated their financial acumen by buying up all your brother's properties. What promotion for you! Your friends are going to look at you with envy in their eyes.'

Mawdo signalled with his hand for me to stop.

'Shut up! Shut up! Stop! Stop!'

But you can't stop once you've let your anger loose. I concluded, more violent than ever: 'Tamsir, purge yourself of your dreams of conquest. They have lasted forty days. I shall never be your wife.'

The *Imam* prayed God to be his witness.

'Such profane words and still in mourning!' Tamsir got up without a word. He understood fully that he'd been defeated.

Thus I took my revenge for that other day when all three of them had airily informed me of the marriage of Modou Fall and Binetou.

19

Aissatou, even in my mourning clothes I have no peace of mind.

After Tamsir, Daouda Dieng ... You remember Daouda Dieng, my former suitor. To his maturity I had preferred inexperience, to his generosity, poverty, to his gravity, spontaneity, to his stability, adventure.

He came to Modou's funeral. In the envelope that he gave Fatim there was a large sum of money. And his look was insistent, saying a great deal – of course.

Where he is concerned, I believe to be true what he used to tell us jokingly, whenever by chance we met again: one never forgets a first love.

After Tamsir, eliminated that memorable day when I quelled his lust for conquest; after Tamsir, then, Daouda Dieng, a candidate for my hand! Daouda Dieng was my mother's favourite. I can still hear her persuasive voice advise me: a woman must marry the man who loves her but never the one she loves; that is the secret of lasting happiness.

Daouda Dieng had kept himself well, compared with Mawdo and Modou. Just on the threshold of old age, he had resisted the repeated attacks of time and exertion. He was elegantly dressed in a suit of embroidered brocade; he remained the same well-groomed man, meticulous and close-shaved. He wore his social success boldly but without condescension.

Although a deputy at the National Assembly, he remained accessible, with gestures that lent weight to his opinions. His lightly silvered hair gave him unquestionable charm.

For the last three years he had commanded attention in the political race through the sobriety of his actions and the precision of his words. His car, with its distinctive cockade in the national colours, was parked on the opposite pavement.

How much I preferred his emotion to Tamsir's confident arrogance! His trembling lips betrayed him. His look swept over my face. I took refuge in banalities: 'How is Aminata (his wife)? And the children? And your clinic? What's it like at the National Assembly?'

My questions came uninterrupted, as much to put him at ease as to renew the dialogue that had for so long been cut off. He replied briefly. But my last question provoked a shrug of the shoulders, to signify 'It's all right,' said challengingly.

I went on: 'It must be all right, that male Assembly!'

I said it teasingly, rolling my eyes round. Eternal woman: even in mourning, you want to make a strike, you want to seduce, you want to arouse interest!

Daouda was no fool. He knew very well that I wanted to relieve him of his embarrassment and to draw back the curtain of silence and constraint that separated us, created by the long years and my former refusal to marry him.

'Still very critical, Ramatoulaye! Why this ironical statement and this provocative epithet when there are women in the Assembly?'

'Four women, Daouda, four out of a hundred deputies. What a ridiculous ratio! Not even one for each province.'

Daouda laughed, an open, communicative laugh, which I found stimulating.

We laughed noisily together. I saw again his beautiful set of teeth, capped with the circumflex accent of a black moustache, combed and very sleek. Ah! those teeth, set close together, had won my mother's confidence!

'But you women, you are like mortar shells. You demolish. You destroy. Imagine a large number of women in the Assembly. Why, everything would explode, go up in flames.'

And we laughed again.

Wrinkling my brow, I commented: 'But we are not incendiaries; rather, we are stimulants!' And I pressed on: 'In many fields, and without skirmishes, we have taken advantage of the notable achievements that have reached us from elsewhere, the gains wrested from the lessons of history. We have a right, just as you have, to education, which we ought to be able to pursue to the furthest limits of our intellectual capacities. We have a right to equal well-paid employment, to equal opportunities. The right to vote is an important weapon. And now the Family Code has been passed, restoring to the most humble of women the dignity that has so often been trampled upon.

'But Daouda, the constraints remain; but Daouda, old beliefs are revived; but Daouda, egoism emerges, scepticism rears its head in the political field. You want to make it a closed shop and you huff and puff about it.

'Nearly twenty years of independence! When will we have the first female minister involved in the decisions concerning the development of our country? And yet the militancy and ability of our women, their disinterested commitment, have already been demonstrated. Women have raised more than one man to power.'

Daouda listened to me. But I had the impression that more than my ideas, it was my voice that captivated him.

And I continued: 'When will education be decided for children on the basis not of sex but of talent?'

Daouda Dieng was savouring the warmth of the inner dream he was spinning around me. As for me, I was bolting like a horse that has long been tethered and is now free and revelling in space. Ah, the joy of having an interlocutor before you, especially an admirer!

I had remained the same Ramatoulaye ... a bit of a rebel.

I drew Daouda Dieng along with my ardour. He was an upright man, and each time the situation demanded, he would fight for social justice. It was not love of show or money that had driven him towards politics, but his true love for his fellow man, the urge to redress wrongs and injustice.

'Whom are you addressing, Ramatoulaye? You are echoing my speeches at the National Assembly, where I have been called a "feminist". I am not, in fact, the only one to insist on changing the rules of the game and injecting new life into it. Women should no longer be decorative accessories, objects to be moved about, companions to be flattered or calmed with promises. Women are the nation's primary, fundamental root, from which all else grows and blossoms. Women must be encouraged to take a keener interest in the destiny of the country. Even you who are protesting; you preferred your husband, your class, your children to public life. If men alone are active in the parties, why should they think of the women? It is only human to give yourself the larger portion of the cake when you are sharing it out.

'Don't be self-centred in your reaction. Consider the situation of every one of the country's citizens. No one is well-off, not even those of us who are considered to be secure and financially sound, when in fact all our savings go towards the maintenance of an avid electoral clientele which believes itself to be our promoters. Developing a country is not easy. The more responsibility one has, the more one feels it; poverty breaks your heart, but you have no control over it. I am speaking of the whole range of material and moral poverty. Better living requires roads, decent houses, wells, clinics, medicines, seeds. I am one of those who advocated that independence celebrations should be rotated annually among the regions. Any initiative that enables regional investments and transformations is welcome.

'We need money, a mountain of money, which we must get from others by winning their confidence. With just one rainy season and our single crop, Senegal will not go far despite all our determination.'

Night fell quickly from the skies, in a hurry to darken men and things. It came through the venetian blinds in the sitting-room. The *muezzin*'s invitation to the *Timiss* prayer was persuasive; Ousmane stood on tiptoe and flicked on the switch. There was a sudden flood of light.

Daouda, well aware of the constraints of my situation, got up. He lifted Ousmane up towards the lamp, and Ousmane chuckled, arms stretched. He let him down. 'Till tomorrow,' he said. 'I came to discuss something else. You led me into a political discussion. Every discussion is profitable. Till tomorrow,' he repeated.

He smiled: neat rows of good teeth. He smiled and opened the door. I heard his footsteps recede. A moment later the humming of his powerful car carried him homewards.

What will he say to Aminata, his wife and cousin, to justify his lateness? ...

Daouda Dieng did indeed come back the next day. But unfortunately for him, and fortunately for me, my maternal aunts

65

were visiting me and he was prevented from expressing himself freely. He did not dare to stay too long.

20

Today is Friday. I've taken a refreshing bath. I can feel its revitalizing effect, which, through my open pores, soothes me.

The smell of soap surrounds me. Clean clothes replace my crumpled ones. The cleanliness of my body pleases me. I think that as she is the object of attraction for so many eyes, cleanliness is one of the essential qualities of a woman. The most humble of huts is pleasing when it is clean; the most luxurious setting offers no attraction if it is covered in dust.

Those women we call 'house'-wives deserve praise. The domestic work they carry out, and which is not paid for in hard cash, is essential to the home. Their compensation remains the pile of well ironed, sweet-smelling washing, the shining tiled floor on which the foot glides, the gay kitchen filled with the smell of stews. Their silent action is felt in the least useful detail: over there, a flower in bloom placed in a vase, elsewhere a painting with appropriate colours, hung up in the right place.

The management of the home is an art. We have learned the hard way, and it is still not over. Even deciding on the menus is not easy if one thinks of the number of days there are in a year and of the fact that there are three meals in one day.

Managing the family budget requires flexibility, vigilance and prudence in performing the financial gymnastics that send you from one more or less dangerous leap to another, from the first to the last day of the month.

To be a woman! To live the life of a woman!

Ah, Aissatou!

Tonight I am restless. The flavour of life is love. The salt of life is also love.

Daouda came back. An outfit of blue brocade had replaced the grey outfit of the first visit and the chocolate-coloured one of the second.

He began right at the doorway, in the same tone of voice as I had used at our first meeting, without stopping for breath: 'How are you? And the children, and your Assembly? And what about Ousmane?' Hearing his name, Ousmane appeared, his mouth and cheeks covered with the chocolate he munched all day long.

Daouda grabbed hold of this little slip of a man, who struggled and kicked his legs about. He let him go with a friendly tap on his buttocks and a picture book in his hands. Ousmane, shouting with joy, ran to show his present to the household. 'No visitors? I shall lead the discussion today ... I from the male Assembly.' He laughed maliciously. 'Don't think that I criticize just for the fun of it. Our incipient democracy, which is changing the situation of the citizen and for which your party may take much credit, appeals to me. Socialism, which is the heart of your action, is the expression of my deepest aspirations if it is adapted to the realities of our life, as your political secretary claims. The openings it has created are considerable, and Senegal offers a new prospect of liberty regained. I appreciate all that, especially when all around us, to our right and to our left, one-party systems have been imposed. A single party never expresses the unanimous view of the citizens. If all individuals were made in the same mould, it would lead to an appalling collectivism. Differences produce conflicts, which may be beneficial to the development of a country if they occur among true patriots, whose only ambition is the happiness of the citizen.

'But enough of politics, Ramatoulaye. I refuse to go along with you, like the other day. I have had my fill of "democracy", "struggle", "freedom" and what have you, all those expressions that

67

float about me daily. Enough, Ramatoulaye. Listen to me, rather. The bush radio has informed me of your refusal to marry Tamsir. Is it true?'

'Yes.'

'I, in turn, and for the second time in my life, have come to ask for your hand ... after you are out of mourning, of course. I have the same feeling for you as I had before. Separation, your marriage, my own, none of these has been able to sap my love for you. Indeed, separation has made it keener; time has consolidated it; my advance in years has purified it. I love you dearly, but with my head. You are a widow with young children. I am head of a family. Each of us has the weight of the "past" to help us in understanding each other. I open my arms to you for new-found happiness; will you accept?'

I opened my eyes wide, not in astonishment – a woman can always predict a declaration of this kind – but in a kind of stupor. Ah yes, Aissatou, those well-worn words, which have for long been used and are still being used, had taken root in me. Their sweetness, of which I had been deprived for years, intoxicated me: I feel no shame in admitting it to you.

Very reasonably, the deputy concluded: 'Don't give me an answer immediately. Think about my proposal. I shall come back tomorrow at the same time.'

And, as if embarrassed by his own revelations, Daouda went away, after flashing a smile at me.

My neighbour, Farmata, the *griot* woman, dashed in after him, excited. She was always trying to see into the future with her cowries, and the least agreement of her predictions with reality thrilled her.

'I met the strong, rich man with the "double trousers" seen in the cowries. He gave me five thousand francs.'

She blinked her deep, piercing eyes that were always trying to probe into mysteries.

'I have given the recommended alms of two white and red cola nuts,' she confessed to me. 'Our destinies are linked. Your shade protects me. You don't fell the tree whose shade protects you. You water it. You watch over it.'

Dear Farmata, how far from my thoughts you were! The restlessness with which I was struggling and which you had foreseen did not in the least signify the anguish of love.

21

Tomorrow? What a short time for reflection, for the decisive commitment of a life, especially when that life has known, in the recent past, the bitter tears of disappointment! I still have a vision of the intelligent eye of Daouda Dieng, the pout of the stubborn lips, which contrasted with the gentleness emanating from his profoundly charitable person, who saw only the best in people and ignored the rest. I could read him like an open book in which each sign was a symbol, but an easily interpreted symbol.

My heart no longer beats wildly in the whirl of the spoken words. I am touched by the sincerity of words, but I am not carried away by it; my euphoria, born of the hunger and thirst for tenderness, fades away as the hours dance past.

I cannot put out any flags. The proposed celebration does not tempt me. My heart does not love Daouda Dieng. My mind appreciates the man. But heart and mind often disagree.

How I should have liked to be galvanized in favour of this man, to be able to say yes! It is not that the memory of the deceased lies heavy within me. The dead have only the weight conceded to them or the weight of the good they have done. It is not that the presence of my young children poses a problem; he could have filled the role of the father who had abandoned them.

Thirty years later, my own personal refusal is the only thing that conditions me. I have no definable reason. Our currents are opposed. Daouda Dieng's reputation for seriousness has already been established.

A good husband? Yes. Public rumour, so wicked and thirsty for gossip where personalities are concerned, has never mentioned any goings-on of his. His wife and cousin, whom he married five years after my marriage out of his duty as a citizen and not out of love (another male expression to explain a natural action), has borne his children. Wife and children, placed by this dutiful man on a pedestal of respectability, offered him an enviable refuge, the outcome of his own effort.

He never accepted any honour without associating his wife with it. He involved her in his political actions, his numerous travels, the various sponsorships for which he was canvassed and which increased his electoral constituency.

Before leaving, Farmata, the *griot* woman of the cowries, had said: 'Your mother was right. Daouda is wonderful. What *guer*[17] gives five thousand francs today! Daouda has neither exchanged his wife nor abandoned his children; if he has come back looking for you, you, an old woman burdened with a family, it is because he loves you; he can look after you and your family. Think about it. Accept.'

All the trump cards! But what do these count for in the uncontrollable law of attraction! So as not to hurt him under my roof, I sent Farmata, the *griot* woman of the cowries, with a sealed envelope for him, with the following instructions. 'This letter must be given to him personally, away from his wife and children.'

For the first time, I was turning to Farmata for help, and this embarrassed me. She was happy, having dreamed of this role right from our youth. But I always acted alone; she was never a participant in my problems, only informed – just like any 'vulgar acquaintance', she would complain. She was thrilled, ignorant of

70

the cruel message she was bearing.

Daouda's clinic was not far from the Villa Fallene. There was a stop for the *cars rapides* just a few metres from his doorstep.

This clinic, set up with a bank loan granted by the state to those doctors and pharmacists who expressed the desire for it, enabled Daouda Dieng to continue practising his profession. He had understood that a doctor could not abandon his call: 'A doctor's training is slow, long, taxing, and they are not two a penny either; they are more useful in their profession than anywhere else; if they can combine their job with other activities, so much the better; but what insensitivity, to give up looking after others for something else!' Thus would Daouda explain himself to our mutual friends, such as Mawdo Bâ and Samba Diack, his colleagues.

Farmata, therefore, patiently waited her turn and, once in front of Daouda in the consulting room, she handed the envelope over to him. Daouda read:

Daouda,

You are chasing after a woman who has remained the same, Daouda, despite the intense ravages of suffering.

You who have loved me, who love me still – I don't doubt it – try to understand me. My conscience is not accommodating enough to enable me to marry you, when only esteem, justified by your many qualities, pulls me towards you. I can offer you nothing else, even though you deserve everything. Esteem is not enough for marriage, whose snares I know from experience. And then the existence of your wife and children further complicates the situation. Abandoned yesterday because of a woman, I cannot lightly bring myself between you and your family.

You think the problem of polygamy is a simple one.

71

Those who are involved in it know the constraints, the lies, the injustices that weigh down their consciences in return for the ephemeral joys of change. I am sure you are motivated by love, a love that existed well before your marriage and that fate has not been able to satisfy. It is with infinite sadness and tear-filled eyes that I offer you my friendship. Dear Daouda, please accept it. It is with great pleasure that I shall continue to welcome you to my house.

Shall I hope to see you again?

Ramatoulaye

Farmata, who had smiled in handing over her letter, told me how her smile soured on her face as Daouda read. Then instinct and observation brought a look of sadness to her face, for Daouda wrinkled his eyebrows, creased his forehead, bit his lips and sighed.

Daouda put down my letter. Calmly, he stuffed an envelope with a wad of blue notes. He scrawled on a piece of paper the terrible words that had separated us before and that he had acquired during his medical course: 'All or nothing. Adieu.'

Aissatou, Daouda Dieng never came back again.

◊

'Bissimilai! Bissimilai![18] What was it you dared to write and make me messenger of? You have killed a man. His crestfallen face cried it out to me. You have rejected the messenger sent to you by God to reward you for your sufferings. God will punish you for not having followed the path towards peace. You have refused greatness! You shall live in mud. I wish you another Modou to make you shed tears of blood.

'Who do you take yourself for? At fifty, you have dared to break the *wolere*[19]. You trample upon your luck: Daouda Dieng, a rich man, a deputy, a doctor, of your own age group, with just one wife. He offers you security, love, and you refuse! Many women, of Daba's age even, would wish to be in your place.

'You boast of reasons. You speak of love instead of bread. Madame wants her heart to miss a beat. Why not flowers, just like in the films?

'Bissimilai! Bissimilai! You so withered, you want to choose a husband like an eighteen-year-old girl. Life will spring a surprise on you and then, Ramatoulaye, you will bite your fingers. I don't know what Daouda has written. But there is money in the envelope. He is a true *samba linguere*[20] from the olden days. May God satisfy, gratify Daouda Dieng. My heart is with him.'

Such was Farmata's tirade on her return from her mission. She thoroughly upset me. The truth of this woman, a childhood companion through the long association of our families, could not hold good for me, even in its logic of concern ... Once more, I was refusing the easy way because of my ideal. I went back to my loneliness, which a momentary flash had brightened briefly. I wore it again, as one wears a familiar garment. Its cut suited me well. I moved easily in it, despite Farmata. I wanted 'something else'. And this 'something else' was impossible without the full agreement of my heart.

◊

Tamsir and Daouda having been rejected, there were no more barriers between the suitors and me. I then watched filing past and besieging me old men in search of easy revenue, young men in search of adventure to occupy their leisure. My successive refusals gave me in town the reputation of a 'lioness' or 'mad woman'.

Who let loose this greedy pack of hounds after me? For my

charms had faded with the many maternities, with time, with the tears. Ah! the inheritance, the fat share acquired by my daughter Daba and her husband and put at my disposal.

They had led the fight for the distribution of Modou's estate. My son-in-law laid down on the table the advance for the SICAP villa and five years' rent.

The SICAP villa went to my daughter, who, with the bailiff's affidavit in hand, listed the contents and bought it.

The story of the Villa Fallene was easy to relate: the land and building represented a bank loan granted ten years ago on the security of our joint salaries. The contents, renewed two years ago, belonged to me, and to support this claim, I produced the receipts. There remained Modou's clothes: those that I recognized because I had chosen and cared for them; and the others ... from the second part of his life. I found it difficult to imagine him in this get-up of a young wolf ... They were distributed to his family.

The jewels and presents given to Lady Mother-in-Law and her daughter were theirs by right.

Lady Mother-in-Law hiccoughed, cried. She was being stripped, and she asked for mercy. She did not want to move out ...

But Daba is like all the young, without pity.

'Remember, I was your daughter's best friend. You made her my mother's rival. Remember. For five years you deprived my mother and her twelve children of their breadwinner. Remember. My mother has suffered a great deal. How can a woman sap the happiness of another? You deserve no pity. Pack up. As for Binetou, she is a victim, your victim. I feel sorry for her.'

Lady Mother-in-Law sobbed. Binetou? Indifference itself. What did it matter to her what was being said? She was already dead inside ... ever since her marriage to Modou.

22

I feel an immense fatigue. It begins in my soul and weighs down my body.

Ousmane, my last born, holds out your letter to me. Ousmane is six years old. 'It's Aunty Aissatou.'

He has the privilege of bringing me all your letters. How does he recognize them? By their stamp? By their envelope? By the careful writing, characteristic of you? By the scent of lavender emanating from them? Children have clues different from our own. Ousmane enjoys his find. He exults in it.

These caressing words, which relax me, are indeed from you. And you tell me of the 'end'. I calculate. Tomorrow is indeed the end of my seclusion. And you will be there within reach of my hand, my voice, my eyes.

'End or new beginning'? My eyes will discover the slightest change in you. I have already totalled up my own; my seclusion has withered me. Worries have given me wrinkles; my fat has melted away. I often tap against bone where before there was rounded flesh.

When we meet, the signs on our bodies will not be important. The essential thing is the content of our hearts, which animates us; the essential thing is the quality of the sap that flows through us. You have often proved to me the superiority of friendship over love. Time, distance, as well as mutual memories have consolidated our ties and made our children brothers and sisters. Reunited, will we draw up a detailed account of our faded bloom, or will we sow new seeds for new harvests?

I hear Daba's footsteps. She is back from the Blaise Diagne secondary school, where she has been representing me in answer to a summons. A conflict between my son, Mawdo Fall, and his philosophy teacher. They clash frequently when the time comes to return corrected essays.

As you know, there is a substantial age gap between Daba and Mawdo Fall, the result of two miscarriages.

This clash, which Daba is trying to resolve, is the third within six months in this form. Mawdo Fall has a remarkable gift for literary work. Right from Form One, he has been top of his class in this subject; but this year for every capital letter forgotten, for a few commas omitted, for a misspelt word, his teacher knocks off one or two marks. Because of this, Jean-Claude, a white boy who has always come second, has moved up to first position. The teacher cannot tolerate a black coming first in philosophy. And Mawdo Fall complains.

This always ends in a quarrel and a summons.

Daba was ready to tell the teacher off, and no nonsense. But I calmed her down. Life is an eternal compromise. What is important is the examination paper ... This, too, will be at the mercy of the marker. No one will have any say over him. So why fight a teacher for one or two marks that can never change the destiny of a student?

I always tell my children: you are students maintained by your parents. Work hard so as to merit their sacrifices. Cultivate yourselves instead of protesting. When you are adults, if your opinions are to carry weight, they must be based on knowledge backed by diplomas. A diploma is not a myth. It is not everything, true. But it crowns knowledge, work. Tomorrow, you will be able to elect to power anyone of your choice, anyone you find suitable. It is your choice, and not ours, that will direct the country.

Now our society is shaken to its very foundations, torn between the attraction of imported vices and the fierce resistance of old virtues.

The dream of a rapid social climb prompts parents to give their children more knowledge than education. Pollution seeps in through hearts as well as into the air.

'Phased out' or 'outdated', perhaps even 'old fogies', we belong to the past. But all four of us were made of stern stuff, with upright minds full of intense questionings that stuck within our inner selves, not without pain. Aissatou, no matter how unhappy the outcome of our unions, our husbands were great men. They led the struggle of their lives, even if success eluded their grasp; one does not easily overcome the burdens of a thousand years.

I observe the young. Where are those bright eyes, prompt to react when scorned honour demands redress? Where is the vigorous pride that guides a whole community towards its duty? The appetite to live kills the dignity of living.

You can see that I digress from the problem of Mawdo Fall.

The headmaster of the school certainly understands the Mawdo Fall–teacher conflict. But you try to side with a student against his teacher!

Daba is here beside me, lighthearted, smiling with all her teeth at a mission successfully accomplished.

Daba does not find household work a burden. Her husband cooks rice as well as she does; her husband who claims, when I tell him he 'spoils' his wife: 'Daba is my wife. She is not my slave, nor my servant.'

I sense the tenderness growing between this young couple, an ideal couple, just as I have always imagined. They identify with each other, discuss everything so as to find a compromise.

All the same, I fear for Daba. Life holds many surprises. When I discuss it with her, she shrugs her shoulders: 'Marriage is no chain. It is mutual agreement over a life's programme. So if one of the partners is no longer satisfied with the union, why should he remain? It may be Abou (her husband); it may be me. Why not? The wife can take the initiative to make the break.'

She reasons everything out, that child ... She often tells me: 'I don't want to go into politics; it's not that I am not interested in the fate of my country and, most especially, that of woman. But

77

when I look at the fruitless wranglings even within the ranks of the same party, when I see men's greed for power, I prefer not to participate. No, I am not afraid of ideological struggle, but in a political party it is rare for a woman to make an easy break-through. For a long time men will continue to have the power of decision, whereas everyone knows that polity should be the affair of women. No: I prefer my own association, where there is neither rivalry nor schism, neither malice nor jostling for position; there are no posts to be shared, nor positions to be secured. The headship changes every year. Each of us has equal opportunity to advance her ideas. We are given tasks according to our abilities in our activities and organizations that work towards the progress of women. Our funds go towards humanitarian work; we are mobilized by a militancy as useful as any other, but it is a healthy militancy, whose only reward is inner satisfaction.'

She reasoned everything out, that child ... She had her own opinions about everything.

I look at her, Daba, my eldest child, who has helped me so admirably with her brothers and sisters. It is Aissatou, your namesake, who has taken over from her the running of the house.

Aissatou washes the youngest ones: Omar, eight years old, and Ousmane, your friend. The others can manage well enough on their own. Aissatou is helped in her task by Amy and her twin sister Awa, whom she is training.

My twins are so similar that I sometimes confuse them. They are mischievous and play tricks on everybody. Aminata works better than Awa. Physically so similar, why are they so different in character?

The upkeep and education of young children do not pose serious problems; washed, fed, cared for, supervised, my own are growing well – with, of course, the nearly daily battle against sores, colds, headaches, in which I excel, simply from having had to struggle.

It is Mawdo Bâ who comes to my aid during the serious illnesses. Even though I criticize him for his weakness, which broke up your relationship, I praise him very sincerely for the help he gives me. Despite his friend Modou's desertion of our home, I can still wake him up, at no matter what hour.

23

My grown children are causing me a great deal of concern. My worries pale when I recall my grandmother, who found in popular wisdom an appropriate dictum for each event. She liked to repeat: 'The mother of a family has no time to travel. But she has time to die.' She would lament when, despite her sleepiness, she still had to carry out her share of the duties: 'Ah, if only I had a bed on which to lie down.'

Mischievously, I would point to the three beds in her room. In irritation, she would say: 'You have your life before and not behind you. May God grant that you experience what I have gone through.' And here I am today, 'going through' just that experience.

I thought a child was born and grew up without any problem. I thought one mapped out a straight path and that he would step lightly down it. I now saw, at first hand, the truth of my grandmother's prophecies: 'The fact that children are born of the same parents does not necessarily mean that they will resemble each other.'

'Being born of the same parents is just like spending the night in the same bedroom.'

To allay the fear of the future that her words might possibly have aroused, my grandmother would offer some solutions: 'Different personalities require different forms of discipline. Strictness here, comprehension there. Smacking, which is successful with the very young ones, annoys the older ones. The nerves daily undergo severe trials! But that is the mother's lot.

Courageous grandmother, I drew from your teaching and example the courage that galvanizes one at the times when difficult choices have to be made.

The other night I surprised the trio (as they are popularly known), Arame, Yacine and Dieynaba, smoking in their bedroom. Everything about their manner showed that they were used to it: their way of holding the cigarette between their fingers or raising it gracefully to their lips, of inhaling like connoisseurs. Their nostrils quivered and let out the smoke. And these young ladies inhaled and exhaled while doing their lessons and their homework. They savoured their pleasure greedily, behind the closed door, for I try, as much as possible, to respect their privacy.

People say that Dieynaba, Arame and Yacine take after me. They are bound by their friendship and willingness to help, as well as by a multitude of similarities; they form a block, with the same defensive or distrustful reactions, before my other children; they swap dresses, trousers, tops, being nearly the same size. I have never had to intervene in their conflicts. The trio has a reputation for hard work at school.

But to grant themselves the right to smoke! They were dumbfounded before my anger. The unexpectedness of it gave me a shock. A woman's mouth exhaling the acrid smell of tobacco instead of being fragrant. A woman's teeth blackened with tobacco instead of sparkling with whiteness! Yet their teeth were white. How did they manage the feat?

I considered the wearing of trousers dreadful in view of our build, which is not that of slim Western women. Trousers accentuate the ample figure of the black woman and further emphasize the curve of the small of the back. But I gave in to the rush towards this fashion, which constricted and hampered instead of liberating. Since my daughters wanted to be 'with it', I accepted the addition of trousers to their wardrobes.

Suddenly I became afraid of the flow of progress. Did they also drink? Who knows, one vice leads to another. Does it mean that one can't have modernism without a lowering of moral standards?

Was I to blame for having given my daughters a bit of liberty? My grandfather did not allow young people in his house. At ten o'clock at night, with a bell in his hand, he would warn visitors of the closure of the entrance gate. He punctuated the ringing of the bell with the same instruction: 'Whoever does not live here should scram.'

As for myself, I let my daughters go out from time to time. They went to the cinema without me. They received male and female friends. There were arguments to justify my behaviour. Unquestionably, at a certain age, a boy or girl opens up to love. I wanted my daughters to discover it in a healthy way, without feelings of guilt, secretiveness or degradation. I tried to penetrate their relationships: I created a favourable atmosphere for sensible behaviour and for confidence.

And the result is that under the influence of their circle they have acquired the habit of smoking. And I was left in the dark, I who wanted to control everything. My grandmother's wise words came to mind: 'You can feed your stomach as well as you please; it will still provide for itself without your knowing.'

I had to do some thinking. There was a need for some reorganization to stop the rot. My grandmother would perhaps have suggested, 'For a new generation, a new method.'

I did not mind being a 'stick-in-the-mud'. I was aware of the harmful effects of tobacco, and I could not agree to its use. My conscience rejected it, as it rejected alcohol.

From then on, relentlessly, I was on the lookout for its odour. It played hide-and-seek with my watchfulness. Sly and ironic, it would tease my nostrils and then disappear. Its favourite hiding place was the toilet, especially at night. But it no longer dared to expose itself openly, with jaunty shamelessness.

24

Today I was not able to finish my evening prayer as I wanted to: cries from the street made me jump up from the mat on which I was seated.

Standing on the veranda, I see my sons Alioune and Malick arriving in tears. They are in a pitiable state: torn clothes, bodies covered in dust from a fall, knees bleeding beneath the shorts. There is a large hole in the right sleeve of Malick's sweater; the arm on the same side hangs down limply. One of the boys supporting him explains to me: 'A motorcyclist knocked down Malick and Alioune. We were playing football.'

A young man with long hair, white glasses, amulets round the neck, moves forward. The grey dust from the road covers his denim outfit. Mauled by the children for whom he has become the target, a red wound on his leg, he is visibly taken aback by so much hostility. In a polite tone and manner, which contrast with his slovenly appearance, he offers his excuses: 'I saw the children too late while making a left turn. I thought I would have a clear road, since it is a one-way street. I did not imagine that the children had set up a playing field. In vain, I tried to brake. I hit the stones marking the goal post. When I fell, your two sons also fell, along with three other small boys. I am sorry.'

I am pleasantly surprised by the young motorcyclist. I railed, but not against him. I know from experience the difficulty of driving in town, especially in the Medina. The tarred surface is a favourite area for children. Once they have taken possession, nothing else counts. They will dance around the ball like devils.

Sometimes the object of their passion is a thick rag ball, all tied up. It doesn't matter! The driver's only recourse is his brakes, his horn, his composure; a small, disorderly opening is made for him, quickly closed up again in the hustle. Behind him the shouts begin again, even louder.

'It's not your fault, young man. My sons are to blame. They slipped away as I was praying. Off you go, young man – or rather, wait a moment while I get you some spirit and cotton-wool for your wound.'

Aissatou, your namesake, brings methylated iodine and cotton. She takes care of the stranger and then of Alioune. The little boys of the area disapprove of my reaction. They want the man 'at fault' to be punished; I give them a ticking-off. Ah, children! They cause an accident and, in addition, they want to punish.

Malick's hanging arm looks to me as if it is broken. It droops unnaturally. 'Quick, Aissatou! Take him to hospital. If you can't find Mawdo, go to Casualty. Quick, go, child.' Aissatou dresses quickly and speedily helps Malick to clean up and change.

The dried blood from the wounds leaves dark and repulsive stains on the ground. Cleaning them up, I think of the identical nature of men: the same red blood irrigating the same organs. These organs, situated in the same places, carry out the same functions. The same remedies cure the same illnesses everywhere under the sun, whether the individual be white or black. Everything unites men. Why, then, do they kill each other in ignoble wars for causes that are futile when compared with the massacre of human lives? So many devastating wars! And yet man takes himself to be a superior being. In what way is his intelligence useful to him? His intelligence begets both good and ill, more often ill than good.

I go back to my place on the mat decorated with a picture of a mosque in green, reserved for my use only, just as is the kettle for my ablutions. Alioune, still sniffing, pushes Ousmane aside so as to take his place beside me, looking for consolation, which I refuse him. On the contrary, I seize the opportunity to tell him off: 'The road is not a playing field. You got off lightly today. But tomorrow, watch out! You will have some bone broken, like your brother.'

Alioune complains: 'But there is no playing field in the area. Mothers won't let us play football in the compounds. So what do we do?'

His comment is valid. Officers in charge of town planning must make provision for playing fields when they are developing open spaces.

Some hours later Aissatou and Malick return from the hospital where, once again, Mawdo has taken good care of them. Malick's plastered arm tells me that the drooping arm had indeed been broken. Ah, how dearly children make one pay for the joy of bringing them into the world!

Just as I thought, my friend: it never rains but it pours. This is my luck: once misfortune has me in its grip, it never lets go of me again.

Aissatou, your namesake, is three months pregnant. Farmata, the *griot* woman of the cowries, very cleverly led me to this discovery. Public rumour had spurred her on perhaps, or her keen powers of observation had simply served her well.

Each time she cast her cowries to cut short our discussions (we had diverging points of view on everything), she would breathe a 'Hm' of discontent. With heavy sighs, she would point out in the jumble of cowries a young pregnant girl.

I had certainly noticed your namesake's sudden loss of weight, her lack of appetite, the swelling of her breasts: all indications of the child she was carrying. But puberty also transforms adolescents; they grow fatter or thinner, taller. And then, shortly after her father's death, Aissatou had had a violent attack of malaria, checked by Mawdo Bâ. The disappearance of her plumpness dates from this period.

Aissatou refused to regain weight, in order to keep her slender figure. I naturally ascribed her light intake of food and her distaste for certain foodstuffs to this new mania. Now thin, she swam in her trousers and, to my great joy, wore only dresses.

Little Oumar did tell me one day that Aissatou used to vomit in their bathroom every morning while bathing him. But Aissatou, when questioned, denied it, said it was the water mixed with toothpaste that she spat out. Oumar no longer spoke of vomiting. My mind focused on something else.

How could I guess that my daughter, who had calmed my anger during the cigarette affair, was now indulging in an even more dangerous game? Merciless fate had surprised me again – as usual, without any weapons with which to defend myself.

Every day Farmata would insist a bit more on the 'young pregnant girl' of her cowries. She would show her to me. The girl's condition was making the woman suffer. She was eloquent: 'Look, I say, look! This separate cowry, hollow side turned upwards. Look at this one, adjusting itself to the other, white side up, like a cooking pot and its cover lid. The child is in the belly. It forms one body with its mother. The two groups of cowries are separated: this indicates an unattached woman. But as the cowries are small, they indicate a young girl.'

And her hand threw down, again and again, the gossipy cowries. They fell away from each other, collided, overlapped. Their tell-tale chink filled the winnowing fan, and the same group of two cowries always remained separate, to reveal distress. I followed their language dispassionately.

And then, one evening, annoyed by my naivety, Farmata said boldly: 'Question your daughters, Ramatoulaye. A mother must be pessimistic.'

Worried by the relentless repetition, anxious, I accepted the proposition. Moving like a gazelle with delicate limbs, she swept into Aissatou's bedroom, afraid that I would change my mind. She came out, a triumphant gleam in her eye. Aissatou followed her, in tears. Farmata sent away Ousmane, who was nestled within my *boubou*, locked the door and declared: 'The cowries cannot always be wrong. If they have insisted for so long, it means there is something there. Water and sand have been mixed; they have become mud. Gather up your mud. Aissatou does not deny her condition. I have saved her by exposing the matter. You guessed nothing. She did not dare confide in you. You would never have got out of this situation.'

I was dumbfounded. I, so prone to chide, was silent. I was flushed and breathless. I closed my eyes, opened them again. I gnawed at my tongue.

The first question that comes to mind on discovering such a condition is: who? Who is behind this theft, for there has been a theft. Who is behind this injury, for injury it is. Who has dared? Who? Who? Aissatou mentioned a certain Ibrahima Sall who, as she talked, very soon became simply Iba.

Bewildered, I look at my daughter, so well brought up, so tender with me, so ready to help in the house, so efficient in every way, so many fine qualities allied with such behaviour!

Iba is a law student at the university. They met at a friend's birthday celebration. Iba sometimes went to meet her at school when she did not 'come down' at lunch time. He had invited her on two occasions to his room in the university halls of residence. She confessed her liking for him! No, Iba had not demanded anything, had not forced her. Everything had happened naturally between them. Iba knew of her condition. He had refused the services of one of his mates who wanted to 'help' him. He loved her. Though he was on a scholarship, he had decided to deprive himself for the maintenance of his child.

I learned everything at one go, from a broken voice

accompanied by much sniffing but without any regret! Aissatou bent her head. I recognized the unvarnished truth of her story. I recognized her in her whole-hearted gift of herself to this lover who had succeeded in uniting in this heart my image and his own. Aissatou lowered her eyes, conscious of the pain crushing me; I remained silent. My hand supported my tired head. Aissatou lowered her eyes. She heard my inner self give way. She was fully aware of the seriousness of her action, considering my recent widowhood, following upon my abandonment. After Daba, she was the oldest of the succession of daughters. The oldest should set an example ... My teeth gnashed in anger ...

Remembering, like a lifebuoy, the tender and consoling attitude of my daughter during my distress, my long years of loneliness, I overcame my emotion. I sought refuge in God, as at every moment of crisis in my life. Who decides death and life? God, the Almighty!

And also, one is a mother in order to understand the inexplicable. One is a mother to lighten the darkness. One is a mother to shield when lightning streaks the night, when thunder shakes the earth, when mud bogs one down. One is a mother in order to love without beginning or end.

To make my being a defensive barrier between my daughter and any obstacle. At this moment of confrontation, I realized how close I was to my child. The umbilical cord took on new life, the indestructible bond beneath the avalanche of storms and the duration of time. I saw her once more, newly sprung from me, kicking about, her tongue pink, her tiny face creased under her silky hair. I could not abandon her, as pride would have me do. Her life and her future were at stake, and these were powerful considerations, overriding all taboos and assuming greater importance in my heart and in my mind. The life that fluttered in her was questioning me. It was eager to blossom. It vibrated, demanding protection.

I was the one who had not been equal to the situation. Glutted with optimism, I had not suspected the crisis of her conscience, the passion of her being, the torment of her thoughts, the miracle she was carrying.

One is a mother so as to face the flood. Was I to threaten, in the face of my daughter's shame, her sincere repentance, her pain, her anguish? Was I?

I took my daughter in my arms. Painfully, I held her tightly, with a force multiplied tenfold by pagan revolt and primitive tenderness. She cried. She choked on sobs.

How could she have lived alone with her secret? I was traumatized by the effort and skill employed by this child to escape my anger whenever she felt faint or whenever she took over from me beside my troublesome youngsters. I felt sick. I felt terribly sick.

I took myself in hand with superhuman effort. The shadows faded away. Courage! The rays of light united to form an appeasing brightness. My decision to help and protect emerged from the tumult. It gained strength as I wiped the tears, as I caressed the burning brow.

Young Aissatou shall have an appointment with the doctor, not later than tomorrow.

Farmata was astonished. She expected wailing: I smiled. She wanted strong reprimands: I consoled. She wished for threats: I forgave.

No doubt about it: she will never know what to expect from me. To give a sinner so much attention was beyond her. She had dreams of sumptuous marriage celebrations for Aissatou, which would compensate her for my own meagre nuptials when she was a young girl, already tied to my steps like a shadow. She used to sing your praises, Aissatou, you who would give her a lot of money at the future wedding of your namesake. The story of the Fiat whetted her appetite and credited you with fabulous wealth. She dreamed of festivities, and here was this girl who had given herself to a penniless student, who would never be grateful to her. She reproached me for my calm: 'You have mainly daughters. Adopt an attitude that you can keep up. You will see. If Aissatou can do "this", I wonder what your trio of smokers will do. Smother your daughter with caresses, Ramatoulaye. You will see.'

I will indeed see when I ask to meet Ibrahima Sall tomorrow ...

25

Ibrahima Sall entered my room at the appointed time. His punctuality pleased me.

Tall, simply dressed. Pleasant features, on the whole. But with remarkably beautiful eyes, velvety, tender in the casement of his long eyelashes. One would like to see them in a woman's face ... the smile as well. I let my gaze rest on the set of his teeth. No treacherous gaps. Without being self-conscious about it, Ibrahima Sall was indeed the embodiment of the romantic young lover. He pleased me, and I noticed his cleanliness with relief: short hair combed, nails cut, shoes polished. He must be an orderly man and therefore without deceit.

It was I who had summoned him, but it was he who started the conversation: 'How many times I have wanted to arrange this discussion, to let you know. I know what a daughter means to her mother, and Aissatou has told me so much about you, your closeness to her, that I think I know you already. I am not just looking for excitement. Your daughter is my first love. I want her to be the only one. I regret what has happened. If you agree, I will marry Aissatou. My mother will look after her child. We will continue with our studies.'

Here then, concise and well said, was all I wanted to hear. How to reply? Should I agree readily to his propositions? Farmata, who was present during the discussion, was looking out for squalls.

She asked: 'You were really the first?'

'Yes,' confirmed Iba Sall.

'Then, warn your mother. We or I shall go to see her tomorrow to announce your crime. She had better save a lot of money to compensate my niece. Anyway, couldn't you have waited until you had a good job before running after girls?'

Ibrahima Sall heard the *griot* woman's remarks without showing any irritation. Perhaps he already knew her well enough by name and character to remain politely silent.

My own preoccupations were very different from those of Farmata. We were right in the middle of the school year. What was to be done to prevent my daughter's expulsion from school?

I told Iba Sall of my fears. He too had given some thought to the problem. The child would be born during the holidays. The essential thing was not to panic, just to let the months go past, and for Aissatou to dress in loose clothes. At the beginning of the following school year the baby would be two months old. Aissatou would then join the final-year class. After this final year, marriage.

My daughter's boyfriend had worked it out logically and reminded me of Daba's clearness of mind.

Ibrahima Sall himself ran no risk of being expelled from the university. And even had he still been at school, who would inform the school of his position as father-to-be? There would be no change in him. He would remain 'flat' ... while my daughter's swollen belly would point an accusing finger.

When will there be a lenient law to help erring schoolgirls whose condition is not camouflaged by long holidays?

I added nothing to all this careful planning. At that moment, I felt that my child was being detached from my being, as if I were again bringing her into the world. She was no longer under my protection. She belonged more to her boyfriend. A new family was being born before my very eyes.

I accepted my subordinate role. The ripe fruit must drop away from the tree.

May God smooth the new path of this child's life.

Yet what a path!

26

Aissatou, reassuring habits regain ascendancy.

My heart beats monotonously under my black wrappers. How I like to listen to this slow rhythm! A new substance is trying to graft itself on to the household.

Ibrahima Sall comes every day and gives each of us what he can. He offers Mawdo Fall his logic and clarity in discussions of the topics of his essays. He provides chocolate regularly for Oumar and Ousmane. He is not too proud to play with Malick and Alioune, who have given up the street for my compound.

Malick's arm is still in plaster. Just as long as his leg, which cannot keep away from the ball, does not break in its turn!

But the trio (Arame, Yacine and Dieynaba) refuse to accept this 'intrusion'. The trio greet him correctly but without enthusiasm. The trio are hostile to his invitations. They begrudge him for having ...

Ibrahima Sall urges Aissatou on in her lessons and homework. He has his girlfriend's success at heart. He does not want to be responsible for any regression whatsoever. Aissatou's marks improve: there's a silver lining in every cloud!

Farmata finds it difficult to accept Ibrahima Sall, whom she describes as 'cocksure', 'shameless'. She never misses an opportunity of hitting out at him: 'Has one ever seen a stranger untie a goat in the house?'

Unperturbed, Ibrahima Sall tries to adapt. He seeks out my company, discusses current events with me, sometimes brings me magazines and fruit. His parents, informed some time ago by the vigilant Farmata, also come round to see us and are anxious about Aissatou's health. And reassuring habits regain ascendancy ...

I envy you for having had only boys! You don't know the terrors I face in dealing with the problems of my daughters.

I have finally decided to broach the problem of sexual education. Aissatou, your namesake, caught me unawares. From now on, I will take precautions. I address myself to the trio, the twins being still too young.

How I had hesitated earlier! I did not want to give my daughters a free hand by offering them immunity in pleasure. The world is upside-down. Mothers of yore taught chastity. Their voice of authority condemned all extra-marital 'wanderings'.

Modern mothers favour 'forbidden games'. They help to limit the damage and, better still, prevent it. They remove any thorn or pebble that might hinder the progress of their children towards the conquest of all forms of liberty! I apply myself painfully to this necessity.

All the same, I insist that my daughters be aware of the value of their bodies. I emphasize the sublime significance of the sexual act, an expression of love. The existence of means of contraception must not lead to an unhindered release of desires and instincts. It is through his self-control, his ability to reason, to choose, his power of attachment, that the individual distinguishes himself from the animal.

Each woman makes of her life what she wants. A profligate life for a woman is incompatible with morality. What does one gain from pleasures? Early ageing, debasement, no doubt about it, I further stressed.

My words fell uneasily on my female audience. Of us all, I was the most vulnerable. For the trio's faces registered no surprise. My chopped sentences aroused no special interest. I had the impression that I was saying the obvious.

Perhaps the trio knew already ... A long silence ... And the trio disappeared. I let out a sigh of relief. I felt that I had emerged into the light after a long journey through a dark, narrow tunnel.

27

Till tomorrow, my friend.

We will then have time to ourselves, especially as I have obtained an extension of my widow's leave.

I reflect. My new turn of mind is hardly surprising to you. I cannot help unburdening myself to you. I might as well sum up now.

I am not indifferent to the irreversible currents of women's liberation that are lashing the world. This commotion that is shaking up every aspect of our lives reveals and illustrates our abilities.

My heart rejoices each time a woman emerges from the shadows. I know that the field of our gains is unstable, the retention of conquests difficult: social constraints are ever-present, and male egoism resists.

Instruments for some, baits for others, respected or despised, often muzzled, all women have almost the same fate, which religions or unjust legislation have sealed.

My reflections determine my attitude to the problems of life. I analyse the decisions that decide our future. I widen my scope by taking an interest in current world affairs.

I remain persuaded of the inevitable and necessary complementarity of man and woman.

Love, imperfect as it may be in its content and expression, remains the natural link between these two beings.

To love one another! If only each partner could move

sincerely towards the other! If each could only melt into the other! If each would only accept the other's successes and failures! If each would only praise the other's qualities instead of listing his faults! If each could only correct bad habits without harping on about them! If each could penetrate the other's most secret haunts to forestall failure and be a support while tending to the evils that are repressed!

The success of the family is born of a couple's harmony, as the harmony of multiple instruments creates a pleasant symphony.

The nation is made up of all the families, rich or poor, united or separated, aware or unaware. The success of a nation therefore depends inevitably on the family.

◊

Why aren't your sons coming with you? Ah, their studies ...

So, then, will I see you tomorrow in a tailored suit or a long dress? I've taken a bet with Daba: tailored suit. Used to living far away, you will want – again, I have taken a bet with Daba – table, plate, chair, fork.

More convenient, you will say. But I will not let you have your way. I will spread out a mat. On it there will be the big, steaming bowl into which you will have to accept that other hands dip.

Beneath the shell that has hardened you over the years, beneath your sceptical pout, your easy carriage, perhaps I will feel you vibrate. I would so much like to hear you check or encourage my eagerness, just as before, and, as before, to see you take part in the search for a new way.

I warn you already, I have not given up wanting to refashion my life. Despite everything – disappointments and humiliations – hope still lives on within me. It is from the dirty and nauseating humus that the green plant sprouts into life, and I can feel new buds springing up in me.

The word 'happiness' does indeed have meaning, doesn't it? I shall go out in search of it. Too bad for me if once again I have to write you so long a letter ...

Ramatoulaye

NOTES

1 An invocation that indicates the seriousness of the subject to be discussed.
2 Form of condolence that also expresses hope of moral recovery.
3 Senegalese food prepared from roughly kneaded millet flour, which is cooked in water and eaten with curds.
4 It is the duty of the husband's sisters to buy his widow's mourning clothes.
5 A drink prepared by mixing sugared curds with well kneaded millet flour; it is cooked in steam.
6 Black African, of any nationality, who is part-poet, part-musician, part-sorcerer.
7 Suburbs of Dakar, capital of Senegal.
8 Sweet-smelling and stimulating powder.
9 Building society in the Cap-Vert department of Senegal (Dakar and environs), which constructs houses for sale or rent.
10 Princess of the Sine.
11 Underground river.
12 Invisible companions.
13 A man in Western-style clothes.
14 Someone who comes from the hinterland; in West African English, 'bushman'.
15 Liquid with supernatural powers.
16 The statutory visit that every polygamous man must make to the bedroom of each of his wives in turn.
17 Nobleman.
18 Beginning of the first *sourate* of the Koran, which has passed into general speech; the expression denotes surprise.
19 Old friendship.
20 A man of repute.